A FORGOTTEN GODDESS

Cecilia Randell

Book One of The Forgotten Trilogy

eBook Published 2018

Print Published 2019

Print ISBN: 978-1-7339745-0-9

Editing by Heather Long and Missy Fournier

Front cover image by Covers by Combs

Published by Blue Wren Publishing

author@ceciliarandell.com

❀ Created with Vellum

Also by Cecilia Randell

The Adventures of Blue Faust

A Girl Named Blue

Behind These Blue Eyes - A Between the Adventures Novella

Beyond Blue Frontiers

For a Pixie in Blue

A Blue Star Rising

Wild is the Blue *(coming May 2019)*

The Forgotten Trilogy

A Forgotten Goddess

The Legends That Remain

The Final Melody

Stand Alone Novels and Novellas

Blinded Beauty

There are so many out there who have supported me. Family, friends, fellow authors. I am eternally grateful to you. For this one…this one is for Faith, without whom this idea would have never been.

Contents

Chapter One

Dearest Bastet,

I'm writing this in the notes application you showed me. There is something wrong with the texting feature of the phone, and I cannot find the one for the emailing. But I do not want to lose these thoughts. I will send them as soon as I have found a computer for my use.

I have made it to the new country, this Ireland, and to the county Sligo. The locals are very interesting, at times gregarious and overly familiar, and at others just like Seth, or even Anubis, turning their chins up in disdain. But not cold, really, they are never cold.

But this place is. Why didn't you tell me to order gloves?

- Bat, the goddess who is damp

BAT SITRU

*B*at shuddered as she pressed through the crowd, her eyes assaulted by the too bright green of banners and streamers despite the half-light of dusk. Cries of greeting and excitement simply added to the offense. The scent of beer wafted from open doors and clutched glasses—and though pleasant in itself—when mixed with something she suspected was cabbage, it had her stomach stirring in revolt.

Many of the storefronts were already closed, though quite a few drinking establishments remained open. *Pubs. They are called pubs.* Streetlights came on and colored safety lights lined the bridge a few blocks away, glinting off the surface of a small river. A brief moment of longing for the swift waters of the Nile filled her.

She'd left her small home near the banks just days before, but having never traveled farther than the next nome—*village*—over, even when her worshipers had extended to Lower Egypt and the delta, she was not used to being surrounded by such... foreignness.

Be honest with yourself, Bat. Even home is no longer home.

A group of revelers passed close on her left, jostling her shoulder bag and half-spinning her.

"Sorry, love!" a man called back to her, then continued on with his friends.

Cold, damp wind blew her dark hair over her eyes as she moved from the center of the walk and closer to the buildings, tugging her case behind her. She needed a moment, just one, to get her bearings. Another blast of air

2

hit her, bringing with it the scent of rain and salt. She wrapped her free arm around her middle and huddled into her inadequate coat.

Gloves. Gloves and boots and a scarf should have been on the list. As thorough as her and Bastet's research had been, they had obviously missed some things. Or the cat was up to her usual tricks. Having a greater mobility—and larger territory—than Bat, the cat knew so much more of this modern world; deliberately putting Bat through a mild torture was exactly something the other goddess would do.

She closed her eyes and breathed in. *Remember why you are here, Bat. Remember. You are needed.*

Bat snorted, softly, a bad habit she'd picked up from Bastet over the centuries. She hadn't been *needed* in millennia. Not since she'd fulfilled the purpose of her creation and helped to unite the kingdoms of Upper and Lower Egypt. After that time, well... No one worshipped the gods as they once had, but she hadn't been sought out, or even remembered, by more than a handful of scholars and explorers over the centuries.

What made her think anything would be different in this land of green fields, cliffs, and damp? A few vague visions and the slim hope that she could help someone, somewhere?

Because you are she of the two faces, who has been saved. A soft and warm breeze accompanied the words, and for one moment she was home on the banks of the Nile, cradled in the arms of Nut the mother sky and supported by Geb the father earth. In that brief moment she was a young goddess, looking hopefully to the years stretched out before her.

And I have saved myself from all things evil. She finished the ancient incantation and opened her eyes. Renewed determination filled her. Her powers may be greatly diminished, but they were *not* gone. She had followed her visions to this place, this Ireland, and she was determined to see them through to the end.

Now she simply needed to find the damned apartment she had rented through the Internet. When a person has traveled over forty-three hundred kilometers and used multiple forms of transportation, you would assume finding one address would be simple. But no. She had acquired a cellular data phone just for this trip, but the map function—*app*—had been showing an error message as soon as she landed in this country. Combine that with the general intoxication level of the residents, the lack of a paper map, and it was the perfect recipe for becoming lost.

Which she was.

Maybe she should have accepted Khonsu's offer of a ride. Days of arduous travel were more than enough to knock down any goddess's pride. But, she had needed to do this on her own. It was important. Standing on her own, even for just a couple months, was the goal; hitching a lift with a moon god was neither of those things.

Curling her toes in her flats and working some feeling back into them, she released the handle of her case and pulled the printed confirmation from her shoulder bag.

45 O'Connell Street, Abbey Quarter North, Sligo, Ireland.

She was close. O'Connell Street should be right in this

area. She hadn't anticipated the country-wide celebrations, though. She knew this new religion had spread widely over the world, and hung on much longer than any of the gods had thought it would, but she hadn't realized the saints garnered such celebration. It was more than many of the old gods received, even in the height of their power.

Her Idiot's Guide had mentioned this Patrick, though it talked more of his story than his worship rituals. In fact, if she weren't so miserably cold, she would have enjoyed celebrating what sounded like an intriguing man, especially with the drinking of beer. She felt a kinship with him and his work of seeking to unite warring peoples of different beliefs.

It was a shame that his efforts had later been ruined. *Just as mine were*. She pulled a lock of her hair and pushed the thought aside. Things that had happened almost five millennia before *did not matter*. And she would continue to remind herself of this until it sunk in.

As she peered around, seeking a street sign or landmark that would tell her precisely where she was, a strange woman with green hair tripped over Bat's case, stumbling into another man who was also just passing. Bat grabbed the handle and pulled her belongings close as the man caught the green-haired woman, helping her regain her balance.

When they both turned to her, Bat stiffened. Their faces were pale, as so many were in this land, and soft. The woman's eyes narrowed and scanned from Bat's straight but tangled black hair, over her plump figure clad in tights and coat, to her inadequately covered feet.

5

"All right, are ya?"

The woman's accent was thicker than the ones Bat had encountered so far, and it took her a moment to sort through her words. "Should I not be asking that of you?" Another gust of wind hit her, and she shuddered.

The woman's expression softened and a kind smile stretched across this stranger's face. She turned to the man. "I'm after thinking she's lost." She turned back to Bat. "Whatever possessed you to travel on Saint Paddy's?" She shook her head and continued before Bat could answer. "Where are you going then?"

"Ailis, don't bother the girl now." The man, with a head of graying hair and carrying a comfortable weight, nudged the green-haired woman to the side, taking her place. "*Are* ya lost?"

Amused at being called a girl, and no longer above accepting help if offered, she answered, "Yes. I am looking for 45 O'Connell Street. I received directions at the transport station, but I have become disoriented."

"Now, Con, don't scare her off." Ailis stepped in front of the man. "I know the place. It's the O'Loinsigh pub. Ye're close. Two streets down and turn right. It's the Dubros. Look for the blue door." Her smile tightened, and Bat grew wary.

Expressions like hers were not unfamiliar and were usually worn by Bastet when the subject of Hathor or Horus came up during a visit. Bat was long over the betrayal that never really was; Horus had never made promises, and neither had Bat. Once more shaking off an old pain that was more of a dull ache, she returned to the present. "Is there something I should know?"

The woman shrugged. "They may no' be open. The O'Loinsighs stick to the old ways."

Bat relaxed. "Oh, that is fine. I am renting the spare room they advertised. I do not mind if the pub is closed."

"Oh, are ya here for a while?" Ailis stepped closer and Bat could see her eyes matched her hair. "Come see me at O'Malley's. We're a bit of a general store, grocer, hardware. We'll have a chat."

Bat smiled and opened her mouth to answer then shivered again, hard.

"And we're keeping you. Ye're near frozen. You come see me, we'll get you set up. Now, just go on down that way." She pointed in the direction Bat had been heading. "Turn right, now, and as I said, it's the one with the blue door." She grabbed Con's arm and tugged. "Come on Con, let's let her be."

Con rolled his eyes, sent Bat a grin, and then allowed Ailis to lead him away. Gazing after them, her mind's eye opened.

Flash. Green hair matted with blood on one side. A pale face stretched into a fierce grin, and a hand gripping a small knife coated in yet more blood.

She strained for more, opening her senses to the stars above. Though they were obscured by the last light of day and the hovering clouds, she could always sense them, no matter how diminished she had become.

They answered with a faint pulse of welcome. But gave her nothing else, and the vision faded to nothing. Whether she saw past or future in that flash she didn't know, but she upped Ailis from an impetuous—though welcoming—local to a possible danger, or an ally.

Shaking off her speculations, she headed along the walk in the direction indicated, only needing to dodge stumbling revelers twice. Following Ailis's directions, she turned right on O'Connell. This street was quieter and most of the shops dark. The light was fast fading in the way of most twilights, and Bat hurried along the walk, scanning the storefronts until she spotted a blue door.

Light spilled through the curtained windows as did voices and music. Trying the knob, she found the door locked. She rapped loudly and sighed, once again clutching her arms around her middle. *So close to getting warm.* She pulled out the printout and compared it to the address plate.

45 O'Connell Street

She studied the ornate and scripted writing on the window front.

The Dubros

Yes, this was the right place. Ailis had warned her they may be closed, but there were obviously people inside. She banged on the blue painted door once more. A light mist settled around her and the chill traveled straight through her bones as she waited. She raised her fist again, ready to hammer it like Seth in a tantrum, when the door was yanked open.

Damn, I wish I was still a fertility deity.

Chapter Two

Bastie,

I met someone tonight. Three someones, to make even Isis jealous. I suspect you know just who I mean.

- Bat, the goddess who is still damp.

BAT

The man before her would have been a *wonderful* offering. That was, if she still accepted those types of offerings and if they were ever brought to her. Those had ceased around the same time all other offerings and sacrifices had tapered off. It was also around the same time Horus had risen to prominence and Seth had fallen fully out of favor.

This man though... Bat sighed and momentarily forgot

the chill. Tall, broad-shouldered, with swirling tattoos peeking out from the pushed-up sleeves of his sweater, he had short dark hair and the shadow of a stubble along his jaw. And his eyes. *Oh, those eyes.* Bright blue, like the lapis of her pendant, and shining from his face.

A scowling face. "What do ya want?"

She blinked. Men were not normally rude to her. Indifferent, yes, but not rude. "I... rented the extra room?" She held out her confirmation.

He glanced down at it and then back up, his gaze roving over her face. "We're closed. Come back tomorrow." He stepped back, hand on the edge of the door and ready to push it closed.

She put forward a foot, blocking him. A trick she'd learned long ago and that came in handy when dealing with Seth and his occasional surliness. It seemed she'd need to brush off those rusty skills quickly in order to deal with her new landlord. "I need a place to stay tonight. I have a confirmation." She held up the paper once more and thrust it toward him.

"Which is for tomorrow." A muscle ticked in his cheek. "It's St. Paddy's. We're closed."

"I understand your worship of this saint is important to you, but I do not believe I can stand another night traveling. I promise if you simply show me to the room, I will not require anything of you until well into tomorrow. I... need to get dry. I have been wet since I arrived." Her shivers increased, and she tucked her hands into her armpits, no longer caring if he took the confirmation. She didn't move her foot, though. She did know better than that.

The man swung the door open and stepped in close enough the warmth of him bridged the gap between them. She was not an insubstantial woman, but he made her feel almost petite. And *warm*. It was not something she had felt since... Bat shook off the stray thought. It wouldn't be a good idea to get involved with anyone at the moment, especially someone as surly as this. She was seeking a new home, and she had two months to decide if this was the place her visions had shown her and if they had shown her the full truth. The flashes had only offered a possibility, after all.

A new figure appeared behind the first man, just as broad and even taller. A neat beard framed his dark face, and he wore his hair slicked back. What caught her attention, though, was the patch covering one eye. It was made of dark leather and bore intricate designs tooled across the surface. His good eye was the same lapis-blue as the first man. *Brothers?*

Her senses stirred, and she braced for another flash, but it didn't come.

"Dub," the second giant said. "What's the issue?" The bass of his voice moved through her like thunder—like storms over the red lands—and she shivered, though not from the cold.

"New tenant is early." Dub shrugged and shifted back, putting a bit more distance between them and taking away his heat.

The second man rolled his eye and slapped Dub's shoulder and without a word turned on his heel, revealing a braid nearly as long as her own hair, and then disappeared back into the pub.

He had... dismissed her. Just as she'd been at home. A hollow pit opened in her belly. It was just as the other gods and goddesses had made her feel. They were not cruel, but without a purpose—and all but forgotten by her own worshippers—she'd often been relegated to the one standing outside the circle and looking in.

Or the one standing on a cold threshold, shivering in a foreign country, while lapis eyes gazed at her mockingly.

Enough. The visions *had* pointed her here. Teased her with the idea of having a new place, and friends. Shown her happiness and contentment. There had been a glimpse of those people *needing* her. There had been a... promise of hope. And no smug *pig* would stop her from finding out if this city could be that place.

Gripping the handle of her case, she shifted right up to the man blocking her path—right on the threshold—and confronted him, her heart pounding. "You will move, and you will show me my room. Now." Bat allowed some of her remaining power to leak into her tones.

Dub's eyes widened and the scowl fell away, replaced by a blankness that was even more foreboding in its own way. Not the reaction she'd expected. There was something there, an echo of something... extra. This was no mere human.

"Of course." He stepped back and to the side.

Pushing her chin up, unwilling to show this not-man that he had intimidated her in any way, she stepped fully over the threshold. There was a pressure, followed by a slight pop and an assault on her senses. Power filled her. For one shining moment the room before her was laid bare. Each person's past, their future, hers to see. The images came, too fast for her to sort.

But wasn't that the way of it? She reveled in the colors, the feelings, the pure life of it. She'd not had a rush such as this in centuries. Longer. The last had been... just before Narmer conquered the Upper Kingdom, and she'd united with Horus and Set to ensure the lands stayed unified and peace reigned. So, much, much longer than mere centuries.

She pushed away the memories attempting to crowd in and let the new visions flow through her. The sorting would come later. Once she'd seen them, the images were hers and came when they were needed, as they were needed. It was the seeing itself that had always been unpredictable.

Oh, don't you now remember, love
When you gave me your right hand
You vowed if you got married
That I should be the man

A voice filtered through the swirls of images, and her attention focused on the far side of the room, and on a man cradling a guitar. He stroked the strings with long fingers, bringing forth a delicate sound.

I wish I were a butterfly
I'd fly to my love's nest
I wish I were a linnet
I'd sing my love to rest

His tenor was smooth and filled the room, carrying over the low conversations of the patrons. He smiled at her, his deep brown eyes merry despite the wistful yearning of the song's melody. Something in his face reminded her of Dub. *So, not a mere man either.*

I wish I were a nightingale
I'd sing to the morning clear
I'll hold you in my arms, my love
The girl I love so dear

She stood before him now, and the room she hadn't really seen fell away until she and this man existed alone. Joy and sadness and something that may have been affection wrapped around her.

The girl I love so dear

The last note faded, and with it those feelings as well. Bat became aware of the smile stretching across her face, matching the man's, and blinked back the tears that had gathered in her eyes. She wasn't even upset that he'd manipulated her so thoroughly. It was deftly done, and she sensed no malice in it, just a wish to share a song. Besides, he'd distracted her from the state of her fingers.

The chair to his left was occupied by a slightly-built, red-haired man holding a fiddle, but the seat to his right was empty. She gestured to it. "May I?"

He gestured to the chair, inviting her to join them. "We've got a bit of a sing-song going. Do ya play?"

"Mell." Dub's voice cut across the room. He still stood near the door, arms crossed and her case beside him.

The musician, Mell, gave a dismissive wave. "It's not a bother. If she's after renting the room, she'll be seeing the bar. She should get to know the patrons, and us." He turned in his chair, angling toward her. "So, do ya? Play?"

"Some. It's... been a while." More like a few centuries since she touched anything other than a sistrum. She missed it. *Then why have I* not *played?* Had her life really become that confined—had she become so limited in *herself?*—she stopped indulging in even the simplest of pleasures? Such as playing any instrument she cared to? *Yes.* "And, it was never anything like *that*," she continued. "That was beautiful. Maybe after my fingers thaw out?"

"Classical training?" he asked, still wearing his smile with ease, though it had gone from joyous to gentle.

She snorted. "Something like that."

"Here." The second man, the one-eyed giant, stood beside her. She'd been too absorbed in Mell to notice his approach. He held a mug out to her, steam rising from the top. "Take off yer coat, it's just keeping ya wet. Have a sit and we'll get ya settled when the night's done."

She struggled out of the coat and traded it for the mug. An earthy yet sweet scent rose from the green-glazed clay, and wonderful heat seeped into her fingers. She took a cautious sip, and that warmth flowed down her throat and spread through her belly. Tea, with a dab of honey, and something more with a bite. It was good.

And this one-eyed man had shown care for her. Had brought her tea without having to be asked or telling her to make it herself. And the third man, the music-maker, had so casually invited her to join in with his friend. Maybe they *were* different from the majority of her own people. "Thank you."

He shrugged. "As Mell said, it's no bother."

"I'm Bat."

That got a small uptick of his mouth. "I know. We rented ya the room. It was on your application."

"Oh." Of course. Heat flooded her cheeks. She'd not been completely isolated over these last centuries. She knew what the Internet was. She read, tried to keep up on the current events of the world. But it was one thing to read of them, and another to experience them. Even such a small thing as filling in information onto a screen, and having it appear thousands of kilometers away seemed something magical, something a god would be able to do —and humans did it every day.

His brows pinched. "Did you not do your research on who you were renting from?"

"Are you not trustworthy?" She raised a brow.

"And you are deflecting." The giant crossed his arms and frowned.

Flash. The giant, a great sword in his hands, blade covered in blood, pieces of gore clinging to the tip. Leather armor protected his chest and tattoos stood out along his arms, stylized animals and circling spirals. He wore a savage expression and his hair hung loose, falling around his shoulders.

Bat took another sip of tea, stalling for time. She'd

known as soon as she crossed the threshold that this place was special, a temple of sorts, possibly. Altogether, it appeared her new landlords were as well. Were they gods as well? Forgotten and diminished as she had been? Or maybe sorcerers, as the ancient priests had been?

"Well?"

"I had a friend help me. I wanted to spend some time in the area. But I haven't... done much traveling. She chose the place, helped me fill out the application." A room with three extremely attractive landlords? Yes, Bastet would see that as a very good idea.

"And you trust her that much?"

"For gods' sake, let her alone. We're not axe murderers, and she's here now." Mell hit a dissonant chord on his guitar. "And tell her yer name already."

The giant ignored his brother. "Well, Bat, it's glad I am you made it to us with no harm. I am Searbhan O'Loinsigh."

"Except you can call him Shar. He's the only one of us to get saddled with a completely unpronounceable name." Mell strummed a new melody and turned to the redhead next to him. "Ready, Dano?"

Bat smiled up at Shar. "I thank you for your concern." It was unnecessary, but she did appreciate it. *He probably needed to... take a chill pill.* It was one of her favorite, recently learned, terms. She'd overheard a young woman on the bus use it to describe another passenger who complained through the whole ride.

Shar gave a short nod, strode through the tables and slid behind a narrow bar set up along the wall to her right.

It was made of a solid slab of scarred wood, stained a deep brown, and polished to a sheen. Shelves of bottles and glasses lined the wall behind it, and a few patrons sat on stools. Others sat at tables dotted around the room, heads bent together. There was even a short set of no more than three booths at the front, near the entrance. An occasional burst of laughter sounded out above Mell and Dano's song. One man sat alone in a corner booth, a pipe hanging from his lips and smoke winding up from the bowl.

Unthinking, she toed off her flats and pulled her legs up, getting comfortable. Dub crossed the room with her case, disappearing through a doorway near the end of the bar and returning a few minutes later without it. The yeasty scents of beer and bread, the bite of alcohol, and the sweet aroma of tobacco lulled her. She continued to sip her tea as her limbs finally thawed.

Her gaze landed on a small harp propped against the rear wall. Her fingers twitched, remembering fingerings and patterns. She rose, her bare feet hitting the rough flagstone floor, and crossed to where it sat near a small hearth. It waited there, for someone—no, the *right* one— to make it come alive again.

She picked it up. Made of a mellow wood that was carved with fish, birds, and spirals, it felt light in her hands. She plucked a string and the tone it made matched the wood—smooth and golden.

She turned back to her seat and Mell watched her, a curiously intent look on his face. Dano shot her a side-eyed glance but kept his chin down, holding his fiddle in place. Neither one broke the melody of their current tune, though she felt their full attention on her. A quick survey of the other patrons yielded either curious looks or quickly averted eyes.

All right. Resuming her seat, Bat ran a finger along the edge of the harp, sending a small pulse of power into it. An answering tingle came back, and the wood hummed. An enchanted instrument then, or one that had been used in many rituals. Well, she was no stranger to these.

Folding one leg under her, she placed the instrument in her lap. She didn't play, not right away. Instead, she listened to the rhythm of Mell's song, and how Dano accompanied him. When she had it, she began.

There were a few false notes and a few missed strings; the spacing was new to her. But she adapted, and soon her song merged with theirs.

When they finished, Mell stared at her, something close to awe on his face. She hadn't seen that expression in far too long.

"Who are you?" he whispered.

"I am Bat."

He shook his head and set aside the guitar, his face hard. There was a warrior side to him now, just as there was in his brothers. "No. I know your name. Who are you? *What* are you?" He paused, but not long enough for her to speak. "You have power. We felt it at the threshold, and it grew as you entered. But you are no fae, nor are you of the clans. And you are not of the Fomoiri, I would know. So, who are you?"

She tilted her head to the side, her hair sliding along her shoulder. The terms he threw out sounded vaguely familiar, though their meanings escaped her for the moment. "I am Bat. That is who I am. I am... I am she of the two faces." *Who was she?* She used to be the Unifier, the peace of the lands. She used to be a fertility goddess and presided over festivals and rites. She used to be an advisor for the kings, showing them the truth of the past and the future. She used to be a guide for the dead, flying with their spirits and reuniting the pieces of their souls. She used to be a nurturer, and a savior, and a guardian against chaos. All these things she used to be, at one time or another.

Now... she was a forgotten goddess, seeking a bit of peace.

His face eased, as though he could sense her thoughts. "Well, Bat, she of the two faces, would you like to play another? You start, we'll follow." He took up his instrument and glanced at Dano, who nodded. Bat didn't get anything from the smaller red-haired man to indicate he was also a diminished god or sorcerer, but surely he must be—they all must be—to be sitting in a locked pub on the night of another holy man's celebration?

The strings of the harp quivered under her fingers, as though asking to be plucked. She started slow, picking out the mostly forgotten tune as it came to her, filling in the missing notes with snips of new music inspired by this land. Her fellow musicians came in slowly, weaving around her melody, supporting it, enhancing it. She closed her eyes and concentrated on the moment.

A voice joined them from across the pub, singing in a language she didn't know, with words that flowed in counterpoint to her melody, blending with Mell's guitar. After another moment a new one, higher pitched and feminine, accompanied it.

She could feel Mell's powers reaching out to both her and the patrons, and she seized upon it. She could sense the balance of it, but also that something was missing. Comfort. And that was something she could provide.

It all came together, and for one shining point in time, she felt at home.

Chapter Three

DUB O'LOINSIGH

*D*ub took his place behind the bar and studied the patrons, looking for signs of unrest or protest against the newcomer. Tonight, they had mostly regulars, minus the humans. In addition, there was a pooka in the corner and a banshee at the bar. He knew them, but not well. They tended to keep to themselves most of the time and rarely came to town.

The girl, Bat, started up another song, his brother and Dano following her lead.

Not a girl, though, is she? If his research was correct, she was a damned Egyptian goddess. He'd tested her at the door, needing to push her into showing herself—her power—if she had any.

Well, he succeeded.

She'd pushed him back. Not physically, but the flavor

of her power was something he hadn't felt in a very long time. It had felt like Brigid, but... not. It was warmer, though somehow distant. As if this being, this woman, was so far removed from the reality of everyday existence that she would slip through his fingers in an instant.

Definitely the taste of a goddess, not a mere immortal, and a far, far cry from the young woman she resembled. That she was Egyptian added both a good helping of anger and a dash of fascination to the situation. He wondered how many of the patrons were of the original immortals to come to Ireland, and just how many of *those* remembered their true origins, and what had driven them from the land of their birth.

He himself was not one, but he'd heard the tales from his father, who'd heard them from his own. Of a land of gods so numerous that all beings other than the humans needed to sustain them were driven from the land. That it had all happened before the great flood—also before his time—had never mattered to his father.

When Bat stepped into the pub and over the threshold, the world shifted. Every single one of the patrons had felt it. Whether it was a shift for the better or not, they would find out soon.

Then she went and picked up the Uaithne, the Dagda's harp. Left at the pub nearly six centuries ago—by the god himself—with the cryptic words "for the Unifier," it had sat there since. For who would dare to touch it? Apparently a nearly nonexistent Egyptian goddess.

No one had expected her to do something so bold, and there had been no time to protest before it was in her hands. Dub had feared a riot when she plucked the first string.

Then she wove her magic, and—based on the current mood—if he tried to take the harp from her now, there would be a different kind of protest.

She used the instrument well, weaving the power of emotion with a skill that not even Mell possessed. She conjured dreams of home, of comfort and warm fires after a long battle fought and won.

She conjured dreams he'd given up too many years ago to count.

The players finished up another song and Bat shifted, tucking her other leg under her and brushing her hair over a shoulder. It fell to her mid back, shining like black silk, dark as the night. Lamplight glinted along it, forming warm stars.

Those same stars shone in her eyes.

Dub rolled his shoulders and dismissed the mawkish sentiment. That was something Mell would put in a song, and not something Dub should ever think of a bedamned *goddess*.

She leaned toward Mell, and her sweater pulled against her round frame, outlining her chest and the indent of her waist. He suppressed a growl as Mell smiled back at her, his cursed charm kicking in.

"You could always go talk to her, you know." Shar stepped up beside him.

Dub tensed. "It was a risk, even letting her in." He hadn't shared with his brothers what his research had found, had wanted to wait until he knew for sure what they were dealing with.

Now it was biting him in the arse.

"Not so much of a risk." Shar poured a whiskey and shoved it in front of Dub. "You had to know she had power when you answered the door. And, it's not so much as to be dangerous."

"There was the flare when she crossed the wards."

"Eh, any who entered for the first time would flare. Especially if they weren't expecting the barrier. Little thing's weak. And you know this place has a buildup, it probably gave her a surge." He poured a glass of whiskey of his own and sipped. "Evened out soon enough."

Dub's lip twitched. Their new tenant wasn't that little. In fact, she had a nice heft to her. Only Shar would call her little. Of course, to Shar, everyone was little. Dub looked back to Bat, the goddess. Bright blue winked at him from the area of her throat. He sensed no malice from her, but his skills had never been with emotion. "She's playing the Dagda's harp."

"And about time someone did." The corner of Shar's mouth turned up. He must be feeling the effects of her song as well.

"Mell's already half in love." Dub was like a lake dragon and his treasure, unwilling to let go of his determination to find fault. Even knowing he did, it didn't stop him.

"Mell's always half in love." Shar refilled the whiskey Dub didn't realize he'd finished. "Dub."

When his brother didn't continue, Dub finally tore his gaze from Bat and met Shar's one-eyed stare.

"She's not Derbforgaill. Or Grainne." Shar's gentle tones grated on Dub's nerves.

The names cut through him. He no longer felt the pain that even the mention of Derbforgaill used to bring, but the betrayal still stung. More so than the actual loss of the woman herself. And Grainne, well, the damage she had done to him was minor in comparison to what she had done to others. "I know that."

"Give her a chance. She's got some power, obviously, but it's faint. Other than playing that long-neglected harp and the flare, she's done naught." Shar's gaze wandered to the dark-haired woman, and his brows drew together. "She didn't even know we were the landlords. Said a friend helped her set up the room. She's not as assured as she seems. Said she hadn't traveled much, and I've a feeling that was an understatement."

Dub's left eyelid twitched. Damn it. He was going to have to come clean. "I did some digging." He leaned on the bar as though resting and sketched a quick rune on the wood for silence. Tricks mostly used by the human Druids, and a skill he'd worked long and hard to master. "She's a goddess."

"Well, I could ha' told ya *that*." Shar's voice deepened.

A small grin quirked Dub's lips, and he kicked his brother's shin. "Not like that. You're as bad as Mell. No, she's a fucking *goddess*. Egyptian. Obscure. Took quite a bit of research."

"Huh. Came up clean on the background check." Shar tilted his head. "Never heard of Bat."

"Course she turned up clean. There was nothing to find." That was the problem. The report *had* been too clean, no tickets, no reports, no fines or schooling records.

27

From Egypt that wasn't so strange in itself. Many of the women were missing records, or never had them.

It was the secondary contact that had sent him searching further. *Bastet, the awesomest Cat of Egypt,* and an email. He'd almost dismissed it as someone having a bit of fun, but an instinct he'd learned never to ignore had prodded him into digging. And it had taken a *lot* of digging.

He continued. "Older. Pre-dynastic. Hard to find much information on her. Doesn't even have any surviving temples." His fist clenched, and the muscles of his forearm tightened. He pushed away from the bar top, careful to keep his power—strength—on a tight leash. They didn't need to be replacing the bar top. Again.

"Explains the lack of power." Shar, calm as always, moved down the bar when Meera, one of the regulars, signaled for another pint. When he was done he came back to Dub's side. "That why you accepted her application?"

Dub shrugged. The same instinct that had insisted he investigate had also insisted they take her in. He didn't have to like it though. "Just wish I knew why she came here."

Now Shar shrugged. "Nothing bad, or the wards would've kept her out. You know that." His expression softened as his gaze moved back to the woman now plucking along to an old Irish ballad, a look of contentment and concentration on her face. His eyelids slipped closed, and he joined in the last line of the song.

And out of the window with another went she.

Dub rolled his eyes. *Why did the Irish have to be so sentimental of tragedy?* He and his brothers had been here so long they had just about fully embraced this quirk, but sometimes it rubbed him wrong. Now, a good battle, he—and the Irish—did love those. These days, though, they were all fought with guns and bombs and no honor. Took the fun right out.

He braced himself and said the last of it. "Some say Bat was the reason Upper and Lower Egypt united. She stood between Horus and Seth and held the peace."

Shar's eye popped open at this. "The Unifier." His words were barely a whisper.

Dub nodded.

The silence between them grew. Then Shar shrugged, his massive shoulders moving as mountains. "You could always *ask* her why she's here."

Why did his brother have to be so calmly logical all the time? Wasn't the youngest brother supposed to be the brash troublemaker? *Hah. That was exactly what he was doing, just in a fashion worthy of a sneaky sidhe.* Dub's eyes narrowed. "Damn you, Searbhan."

His brother just grinned at him.

MELL

Mell smiled at Bat, probing her emotions, trying to get a better read on her. He couldn't truly get thoughts, never had been able to, but he could glean quite a bit from the scraps of emotion that always leaked from a being.

29

Even a goddess.

Mell had figured it out. It must have been *this* that made Dub so jumpy—and more than surly—over the last weeks. His brother had been in charge of vetting the renter. Mell had stumbled on his notes, too, but they were ambiguous. Now he knew what "representation of the milky way" meant. It was the damned stars in her eyes. Add in the fact she could play the Uaithne, that she would think almost nothing of picking it up in the first place, confirmed it for him.

And now that he'd met her, he knew the precise reason Bat was here.

She was lonely.

He continued to pick out the melody, Dano's fiddle following him while Bat worked to keep up. The sweet tones of the Dagda's harp filled the pub, easing worries and troubles. He could feel old resentments fade away under the gentle notes.

Comfort.

And that was Bat's contribution.

She was beautiful. Dark and soft. Something a man could sink into, could lose himself in. She would cradle him and ease away the pain. How the gods of her land would let her up and leave like that he didn't know, but he was glad for it.

The color returned to her face, a warm and deep flush along her golden cheeks. Everything about her spoke of foreign lands and exotic adventures, the kind he hadn't been on in far too long. The last…

He shoved aside the memories. He didn't think of that time, ever. His life had achieved a delicate balance, and he was careful to keep it. Mell focused on the now. Always on the now.

Maybe, if his brother didn't interfere, he would be able to explore these new lands that appeared before him.

He slipped a tendril of longing, and then another of desire, into the melody.

Bat's fingers tripped over the strings and stilled. She stared at him wide-eyed for a bare second then her eyes narrowed. She hit a discordant chord, cutting off Mell's power.

It was his turn to falter.

He shot a quick look at the patrons and noted the wide grins. They hadn't missed the byplay. Based on the scowl Dub wore, he hadn't failed to notice it either.

Damn. There would be a lecture later.

He put out a bit of amusement, and a gentle affection, soothing the scene back into the light playfulness of earlier.

The night continued like this. For the next three hours, they played. The banshee joined in sometimes on a pair of pipes she brought with her. Old Mike sang as well. The will o' the wisp had a good voice. Shar brought their new goddess another whiskey-laced tea, handing it to her with an overly gentle hand.

Looked like she was weaving a spell on more than just Mell.

Finally, it was time to close up and for the customers to be on their way. Mell said goodbye to Dano, promising the little man he'd come to see him the next day and settle payment on their joint... project. Dub locked the door behind the last patron and lowered all but the lights behind the bar. They'd finish the cleanup in the morning.

Mell glanced at Bat where she sat in her chair, lids drooping. She swayed slightly, and he rushed to her side, chuckling. "Here now, let's get you to bed, shall we?"

"Not yours," she said and yawned.

"Certainly not. I would want you awake when you come to my bed." He held out his hand.

She sent him a sleepy glare but accepted his help. He pulled her to her feet and led her to the narrow hall leading to the back stairs. When they reached the top, she stood there waiting for direction.

"Third door to the left. Room faces the canal. Can't really call it a river, though some do." He kept his voice soothing.

She blinked at him and headed left. When she went past the door, he grabbed her elbow and pulled her back. She stared at the knob until he reached out to turn it, gently pushing the door open. He gave her a small shove to get her moving, then guided her to the bed and watched as she fell into it. Grinning, he slipped off her flats and spread a comforter over her.

"Sleep well, Bat of the two faces. Welcome to Ireland."

Chapter Four

Bastet,

I am beginning to suspect none of what I have to tell you will come as a surprise.

This pub is an intriguing place. They gather like family and sing cheerful songs of battles and loves lost. It is quite the contradiction. One of them, the big one like a pirate, made me a wonderful type of tea. I will see if I can find what kind it is and send you some. You would like it.

- Bat, the goddess who has strawberries.

BAT

*B*at stretched under the fluffy comforter that covered her. It wasn't very heavy, but it had kept her snug through the night. She vaguely recalled Mell leading her up the stairs and to the bed. Last night had been amazing. Well, after she had warmed through it had been amazing. She hadn't had fun like that in too many years.

Stretching out her arms, she flexed her fingers, feeling a twinge of soreness; but it was the soreness of well-used muscles, and of accomplishment, and she didn't mind it one bit. Yawning, she pulled her arms back in toward her chest and snuggled into her pillow. She tried to recapture her dream, one of strong arms and music, but it eluded her.

A horn honked, and a car door slammed on the street below, the sound carrying through her window. A faint clanking, followed by a soft chime, filtered through her window. A shouted greeting and another slamming door came next.

The world stirred and so must she.

Pausing for a few seconds more to enjoy the fluffiness surrounding her, she eventually pushed back the cover only to find she still wore the tights and sweater of yesterday. She blinked crusty eyes and licked over her teeth.

Was it improper that the power she missed most of all was the one that did away with the need to constantly manually groom herself? Mornings were the time she felt the most human. *What is the use of being a goddess if you still had to brush your hair and teeth regularly?* She sniffed. *And wash under your arms.*

She sat up and crossed her legs. This must be her room; at least, there was no one else in it, and there were none of the intimate touches a person put on a place they considered theirs.

It was small, but snug. The walls were a light rose with accents of bright blue. Sunlight filtered through cream-colored curtains that covered the windows beside her bed and along the right wall, and thin rugs were placed in strategic spots on the wooden floor. A tall dresser stood against one wall, and a low side table had a place to one side of the bed. There were two doors: one opposite the bed and currently closed, the other beside the dresser, open a crack and through it, she could see shining white tile and a mirror.

It matched the pictures from the Internet exactly.

Best of all, it was warm.

Spotting her case against the wall on the other side of the dresser, she pushed aside the urge to remain right where she was for the rest of the day and rolled out of bed.

Time to get started on her new life, and see if she could find out just what the cat had landed her in.

Clean and in her warmest clothes, Bat pulled open the door of her room and peeked out, looking up and down the hall. It was narrow, with grooved wood wainscot and a flower pattern on the walls. There were four closed doors, the other two on her side of the hall and two more opposite, but no brothers.

She took a deep breath and slowly let it out. She hoped they didn't ask her to find another place, but after last night she wasn't so sure they wouldn't. Mell seemed to like her, but Dub hadn't stopped scowling in her direction from the time she stepped into the pub. Shar was harder to read, but she hoped the fact he kept bringing her that lovely tea-with-a-bite indicated he welcomed her.

She'd made it halfway down the stairs when low voices and the clink of glass reached her. She followed the sounds through a doorway and into the pub. It looked different in the light of day, somehow both more and less magical. And though not nearly as old as her destroyed temple, she could feel the age of the place.

The three brothers worked around the room. Mell swept, shifting chairs to get under the tables. Dub was behind the bar, wiping down the counter and shelves. Shar stood at the far end, sorting bottles and glasses into a large sink.

They carried out the actions with no fuss, no protest or groaning. Their limbs moved in graceful motion, efficient.

"Can I help?" The words left her before she knew she'd had the thought.

Three heads lifted in unison and turned to her. There was one long pause, and then Dub spoke. "No. You are a paying tenant. In fact, you're paid up for the next two months. There is no need for you to work here."

"Oh." There was a twinge in her chest. It was not that she wanted to engage in menial labor, but she *had* wanted to help. To make the offering in thanks for the warm welcome.

Mell shot a dark look at his brother and set aside his broom. He crossed to her, stopping far enough away that she didn't need to crane her head back. "Did you sleep well?" His mellow tones eased her disappointment.

She raised a brow. "You should really stop doing that."

Shar let out a short laugh and joined his brother in front of her. "You can tell when he's pulling the strings, can't you?" Grinning, he slapped his brother. "She's got ya now."

"Ummm... yes, I can tell. And I appreciated it last night. But I do not approve of constant use. If you do it too much, you'll forget what is real."

Mell's eyes narrowed while Shar smirked. The taller brother looked like a... rogue. Like one of those pirates on the romance books Hathor liked to order. Bastet would sneak a couple to Bat every few months, whenever she didn't think they would be missed. They were entertaining, though Bat often found the heroines to be very silly.

"How did you get so wise, little goddess?" Mell's voice was smooth and low; sound alone. He had pulled back his power.

What did he mean, wise? "It seems to be common sense to me. And I am not as young as I look." She gave him a smile, seeking to take any sting from her words. *Also, goddess?* "You know of me? I thought too many had forgotten..." She trailed off, looking between the two brothers, unsure of what she sought.

Mell tilted his head to the side. "We are not idiots."

"And we are not as trusting as some." Shar sent her a pointed look. "Dub did his research before you even got here."

"Then you knew all along? Why the hesitation in letting me in?" Anger stirred. She'd been *cold*.

"Get back to work." Dub's steely tones carried from behind the bar. His brothers shrugged and, sending her parting smiles, went back to their chores. "Bat, we'll be about half an hour. Then we'll discuss arrangements for your stay with us and... other things. If you'd like, there's a small cold breakfast laid out for ya in the kitchen."

He sounded enough like the father earth, Geb, at his most disapproving that for one moment Bat wanted to stick out her tongue and stay where she was, simply to be disagreeable. But, she *was* hungry. She shrugged and turned away, intent on finding this kitchen and the food Dub promised her. Maybe she could get Shar to make more of that wonderful tea when they came to her.

She located the kitchen on the lower level, the door tucked beside a small room with cleaning supplies and a stacked washer/dryer. She sighed. What was the world coming to that a goddess knew how to do her own wash? Or what a stacked washer/dryer looked like?

The kitchen, like her room and the halls, was small. Cabinets wrapped around two walls in an "L" shape. A gas range sat on one end, and on the other was a porcelain sink under a window. An open pantry held dishes and cans of food.

In the middle, a wood-topped island stood with pots and pans hanging from the underside and a sliced loaf of bread on top. Beside this sat butter, jam, and a small bowl of fruit. She inhaled, taking in the scent of fresh bread.

Maybe Dub wasn't so bad.

She plucked a strawberry from the bowl and popped it into her mouth, moaning at the tart sweetness. So much better than the ones grown at home. She grabbed a slice of bread and spread butter over it, biting in before she was even done chewing the fruit.

Wonderful.

Licking a smear of butter from her top lip, she looked out the window. Expecting to see a busy street with rushing pedestrians, she instead found a small garden. Only a couple of meters wide, it spanned the space between the pub and the next building. Neat rows of green rose from raised beds. One corner housed a tangle of brambles, blueberries dotting the branches. Beside those were a few bushes with red berries.

It was such a little thing, a small detail, but excitement moved through her. *Did that mean she could have strawberries every day?* She would do *dishes* if she could get strawberries every day.

She shifted and craned her neck, hoping to see into the far corner. She caught a glimpse of deep red and pale pink but couldn't quite make out what stood there. Disappointed, she moved away from the window. Then it occurred to her. She could go outside. She *should* go outside. There was absolutely nothing stopping her from exploring this new place.

What is that saying? Old habits die hard?

Her days of sitting in her temple, waiting for visitors, waiting for supplicants, waiting for the other gods to seek her out—to include her—were over. Now, if she wanted to explore a mini-garden, there was no reason she shouldn't.

Grabbing a couple more berries from the bowl, she headed for the door on the back wall. Surely, she could find a way to the garden from there.

She reached for the knob, but a new sight drew her attention. A pair of boots sat directly before the door, too small to belong to the brothers. Made of brown leather, they had a sturdy sole, and blue accents swirled along the top. Shoving the berries into her mouth, she crouched down and ran a finger over the arch.

Were they for her? Delighted, she slipped off her flats and pulled the boots on. They were a little loose, but with thick socks, the fit would be perfect. *I should probably be wary of offerings and gifts in a strange place.* But she sensed no curse upon them, no... geas—another word she'd picked up in the Idiot's Guide.

She bounced to her feet and pulled open the door.

She was out on the stoop and about to take her first step down the short flight of steps to the alley when she saw the body.

Chapter Five

Bastet,
The people here are very strange. They are gods but not.
One of the smaller ones, a cheerful man who played the
fiddle, was killed. I am going to help catch the killer.
Also, my visions seem to be coming faster and are getting
more detailed. You may have been right; this may be a good
place for me.

- Bat, the goddess who is warm but very, very angry

BAT

*B*at sucked in a breath, one foot frozen in mid-step. It was Dano, the small red-haired man from last night. The one with whom she'd made music. He lay sprawled, half in the alley and half on the bottom two steps of the stairs.

He was not a god after all.

She didn't need to check if he was alive, she could feel that his ka—his body spirit—had already departed. Tears gathered in her eyes as she opened her mind's eye. Even his flying spirit was gone. It should have been here, hovering, lingering upon the air, waiting to reunite with its other half and proceed on the journey to judgment and the otherworld. But she could sense nothing of it, and there would be no uniting the parts. Just to be sure, she sat on the first step and reached for his arm, seeking any lingering traces of his soul. Sometimes touch helped, provided the physical connection the soul craved, and that kept it in the vicinity until the ka could return.

No, the body was empty.

"What did you do?" The growled words were followed by a harsh grip on her shoulder, yanking her from the body.

Flash. Dub, standing on the prow of a ship. A fierce grin stretched across his lips. Behind him stood Shar and Mell. All were clad in leather and furs, the wind blowing back their long hair.

Flash. Dano in a dark alley standing opposite Mell. Dub behind his brother and slightly to the side. Dano pulling out something small and partially wrapped in a light cloth. A glint of gold as Mell took it from him.

Flash. A delicate hand, skin pale with a small trace of freckles, gripping a short double-edged blade that glowed with a dark light, the pommel of the hilt a serpent's head. It slid into a belly covered in a deep red coat.

Flash. The alley again. Green hair and light red, ducking around a corner.

Flash. Dub, frowning in concern. A hand, calloused and scarred, reaching for her face, cradling her cheek.

"What happened?" Mell's voice broke through the visions and Bat blinked. Her gaze locked with that of Dub's, his face inches from hers. The lapis of his eyes shone below brows drawn together in... worry?

"Is that Dano?" Shar's rumble came from inside the kitchen. There was no more room on the stoop.

"Shit, Dub, get her inside." Mell reached for her arm and she flinched, not wanting to bring on any more visions just yet.

The skin around his eyes pinched and he halted, his hand hovering in the air. Bat didn't want to hurt him, but she needed a moment to process the visions before any more came to her. She'd had more while in contact with these men than in the last century.

She looked back to Dub. "I am fine. I wanted to explore the garden and found him like this. I wanted to do what I could to comfort his spirit." She frowned, disturbed once again by the lack of a soul. "It wasn't there. It shouldn't have been gone so quickly, even without the proper rituals. It didn't linger at all." She turned her head and stared at Dano, lying there, still and silent, the red of his hair clashing with the red of his coat.

The red of his coat. "Was he stabbed?" The words came out soft and detached. She shivered in the early morning air, but she didn't feel the cold or the damp at the moment, preoccupied as she was with this mystery.

Dub cupped her cheek in one rough hand and directed her gaze back to his. His frown remained. *He's always frowning.*

Flash. Dub, smiling with warmth, the lapis of his eyes glowing with affection. He mouthed a name.

Bat's muscles locked. That expression—the longing of it—nearly broke her heart, though she couldn't hear the name he uttered. What was it? Why would she see such a vision?

And why did she care so much about what made this man smile? It should matter nothing at the moment.

"*Are* you okay?" His tone demanded an answer.

She swallowed. "Why is his ba—his flying soul—missing? Also, he's wearing a red coat."

"Dammit, she's loopy. Get her back inside. We need to call the Ceilte Guardi." Mell reached for her again, and she shifted back once more.

Her powers were building quickly, and she needed to get over centuries of no practice. Fast. "I'm fine. Or, I will be." She pushed to her feet, and Dub rose with her. Her shoulder brushed against his chest, sending a small thrill through her middle. A *few* things were out of practice.

Maybe Bastet *was* right. Ireland would be good for Bat.

But first, there was a mystery to solve. Was this how she was supposed to help? Dano didn't deserve to die a second death so swiftly, with no judgment rendered, no chance at the otherworld.

She tilted her head back and met Dub's gaze once again. "I think I can help. But, first, can I get some more of that tea? It was very good. And I'm cold again despite my new boots. Thank you for those." She concentrated on these small things, using them to steady her thoughts, and calm the anger that was beginning to churn in her middle.

Dub glanced at her feet, his mouth thinned, and he nodded. Mell grinned, but it was tight, and he kept sending sneaking glances at the body. She peered past them both to glimpse Shar heading for the kettle on the stove.

~

SEARBHAN

Tea.

She wanted the tea. Tea with whiskey.

I can do that.

He couldn't make the body disappear or erase that sadness from her eyes, but he could certainly make her tea.

Oh, Dano. What did you get yourself into now, you dirty old leprechaun?

And what was he doing on their back stoop?

Shar set the kettle to boil and strode back to the pub, grabbing his favorite whiskey from the top shelf. He set out a mug, the tea bag hooked inside, and added a dollop of honey, just as he had the night before. Three times the night before.

Dub and Bat entered the kitchen as the kettle went off. Dub continued into the hall and returned with a stool from the bar. Setting it down at the island, he gestured for Bat to sit.

Shar busied himself with getting the proportions of tea to whiskey just right. He kept an eye on Dub though, noting how even though his brother frowned, he was very much solicitous of the little goddess's comfort. Almost gentle, or as gentle as Dub ever got.

Interesting.

Shar himself felt the draw. There was something about her, something that called to him even before she picked up the harp. Seeing her shivering at their door last night, he'd had to walk away before he pulled his brother out of the way and swept her into the pub. Into his arms where he could protect her.

Protect a goddess? Now you're getting above yourself Searbhan. You couldn't even protect a tree. Admittedly, it was a sacred tree, and there were many people after the rowan and its berries, but still.

He glanced out the window, looking upon his garden. It gave him a measure of solace, as always. Stirring the tea, he sent out a bit of power to the raised bed where the carrots were looking a little wilted. A hint of pink in the corner caught his eye and he frowned. *Those roses shouldn't be blooming yet.*

Another mystery, though not one as immediate as the body on their rear stoop. He raised the mug of tea to his nose and sniffed. *Perfect.* A small offering for his—*not his* —little goddess. She could use the boost a few offerings would give her. They'd have to be careful, though, the deities of the area could be territorial, and he didn't want Bat getting in trouble.

Turning to hand her the mug, he spied the boots on her feet. Boots she didn't have last night. Boots that he knew didn't exist before this morning.

Another offering.

Oh, Dano.

Sorrow moved through him, a sweet pain. The leprechaun had probably worked on those all night, something to show his appreciation for the music and companionship she'd given them all.

He set the tea before her and watched as she cupped the mug in her hands, sipped, and sighed, her eyes closing briefly. He wondered if she could feel the care he'd put into it. How did a goddess measure an offering? What was the value calculated against?

And why was he worried about a cup of tea while Dano lay extinguished from this life?

Shar ran a hand over his hair and down his braid. Unlike his brothers, he refused to cut it. It was his past, and there was no avoiding that. Why pretend? He met Dub's gaze with his good eye. "Mell calling the guardi?"

"Yes, he'll stay out there till they get here."

It was a good plan, Mell dealt with them the best of the three brothers, but Shar could wish he was here to help with the emotions choking the air.

Dub stepped up to the edge of the island and placed his hand on the wood top, centimeters from where Bat's elbow rested. His fingers curled in and then flattened out. Slowly, carefully.

Dub, always so careful of his strength. The irony had never been lost on them. The giant brother, born with an affinity for growing things, and the eldest who held strength unimaginable.

Shar stepped back and leaned against the sink cabinet, crossing his arms.

After another sip, Bat set the mug down but didn't release it. "I can help."

He noted her slight shiver and suppressed the impulse to pull her into his arms. He could definitely keep her warm. Maybe he could offer himself up for the task? If she accepted…

And now I sound like Mell.

"How?" Dub's voice was harsh, but there was an underlying grief for a departed friend. It never mattered how long you had lived, or the trials you had experienced before, the loss of a friend was never easy.

Tilting her head, Bat peered at Dub from the corner of her eye. Her lips thinned then slowly relaxed. "The visions." She licked along her bottom lip and Shar watched, fascinated by every small movement. "They are not as clear as they once were, but I was able to glean a few things. And… there may be more."

"Visions?" Shar dropped his arms and straightened, attention no longer on those lips. Well, mostly.

Bat's gaze settled on him and then bounced back to Dub as the sharp sound of cracking wood came from under his fist. A small split traveled over the island surface. She closed her eyes and took a breath, her breasts pressing against the weave of her sweater. A small amulet hung from a delicate rope of gold, a bright blue stone carved in the shape of a cow's head with stars topping each horn. She'd worn it last night as well, but it had been hard to see in the low light.

Her eyes opened and locked on Shar. Her chin rose minutely in defiance, but there was a reserve in her face he didn't like. "Yes. The visions. They are diminished, as I am. But they are still there, as I am still here." Her eyes swirled, and Shar could see a whole universe there. "For I am Bat, the unifier of the kingdoms. I am Bat of the two faces, of the black lands of the river and the red of the sands. I see the past and the future, and I help to guide the souls that fly into reunion with their pieces. I maintain the balance. I am the One Who Is Saved, and I have saved myself from all things evil."

Shar's muscles locked and he swallowed. His blood surged and pooled in his groin.

Then her eyes dimmed. She sent him a small smile. "Or, I used to be. I also used to be a bit of a fertility goddess." Her gaze flicked to his pants and her smile grew into a smirk. "But, that was *long* ago." She turned to Dub. "I am not an idiot. I know you are not mere humans. Therefore, you must have some idea of who I am. You said as much yourself earlier. So, yes, visions. I saw some of what befell Dano. Much of it did not make sense, but it often does not, not until the pieces are compiled. I will share what I saw." Her expression hardened. "And we will find out who would do something so atrocious as to give that small man the second death and bar him entrance to the otherworld."

Chapter Six

MELL

*M*ell crouched over Dano's body and cursed. Bat was worried about some nonsense with souls. Well, Mell was worried about the fact that Dano was *dead*.

There were two ways an immortal could die: voluntarily passing on to the Otherlands, or being mortally wounded by a soul blade—one of the *lann de anam*. Dano did *not* pass on to the Otherlands, which meant someone was out there with a gods damned soul blade. Which in turn meant a shit storm was about to descend on his small home.

He reached for Dano's shoulder and hesitated. The Ceilte Guardi—those warriors who elected to become the peacekeepers and investigators during times of peace, much like the modern police—would be able to tell if he touched or moved the body; on the other hand, he wouldn't be able to examine the scene in full after they got here.

Cursing, he stood and pulled out his cell. He dialed the number for the only person he had a hope of getting cooperation out of.

"Cumhaill here." The smooth tones held a hint of the arrogant war leader Finn used to be.

"Well, an' now there ya are." Mell couldn't resist layering on the brogue.

"Mell." Fondness mixed with not a little exasperation. "Hold on."

Muffled voices and a bang traveled over the line. A couple appeared at the mouth of the alley and moved on, pedestrians out on errands, or maybe getting in a stroll. Mell cursed and sketched a quick rune of concealment. Stupid. *Distracted*, he admitted to himself.

Finn came back on the line. "Have you finally come to your senses?"

"Never." He injected a good amount of mock horror into the word and added a shudder, though Finn couldn't see him.

"Well then, if you are not after accepting my offer of a spot in the unit, why are you calling me?"

Back to it. He sobered. "Dano's dead."

Silence. Then, "Dead?" Finn's voice grew smoother, if that was possible.

"Aye." Mell swallowed as clouds obscured the sun. Another Irish shower on the way. His gaze snagged on the red of Dano's coat and for a moment he was no longer in a back alley, but on a field of battle, pain surrounding him, seeping into his being. He cleared his throat. "I want you on this one."

"I can't make that call. You know that."

"He's lying on me back stoop, Finn. And there's a... complication." A memory of the night before, and a pair of large brown eyes, drove out the echo of a war long done. A good complication to be sure.

"Did you—"

Mell cut him off. "No."

"But there's a complication."

"Other than the fact he's *dead*? Yes." Mell crouched beside Dano once more.

"I'll see what I can do."

"Good. Because I'm going to examine the body."

"Goddess damn it, Mell, don—"

Mell disconnected and slipped the phone into his back pocket, his gaze focused on Dano. He opened his mind and reached out, with both his hand and his power.

He sorted through the lingering traces of emotion. It was not something he did easily, or often, but he was one of the few Fomoiri who could. Most of his race had a more physical connection to the world, like Dub and his strength and Shar with his plants. They stuck to the seas where they had an uneasy understanding with Manannan mac Lir, or the hills and rocky shores where their skills were advantageous and went more easily unnoticed.

Emotion and spirit were usually the domain of the Tuatha and the fae races, though of course there was some crossover. He snorted. The peoples of Ireland had been mingling for so long now that "race" was more a matter of power traits and which family you were born into than anything else. Fomoiri, fae, Tuatha, sidhe... pretty words for the same thing, really. Banshees still wailed, pookas still played their tricks and will o' the wisps still got people lost and stuck in the bogs. But unless it never looked human and never would, well, who cared?

His particular ability was one of the reasons Finn continued to try to recruit him into the guardi. It also served to drive his Da a little mad. Alatrom never got over the speculation that Ma had stepped out on him, and relations there were strained to say the least.

He pulled back from the body, processing what he'd felt. Sorrow, guilt, and... love? He turned Dano over. A stain, darker than the red of the leprechaun's coat, spread over his belly.

Bat's words came back to him. *Was he stabbed?* He'd not thought much of it, because of course Dano had been attacked with a soul blade if he was dead. But why would she need to ask?

He rolled Dano back onto his stomach. His left arm flopped against the stairs, and a light *ting* rang out. A small object, glinting gold, bounced down the steps and into the alley.

Checking that he was still unobserved, Mell fetched it. It was a ring, a Claddagh, and small, made to fit a woman's finger. He probed with a bit of his waning energy. Love, affection and... that was it.

Oh, Dano. He turned back to the body and placed the ring back in the lifeless hand, curling the fingers around it. He wondered who the woman was that the ring had been intended for.

Just as Mell stepped away, the sound of boots

pounding on concrete reached him. A group of four Ceilte Guardi rounded the corner and entered the alley. A large man led them. Hair that was more red than gold was shorn close to his head and almost obscured by the uniform cap. His coat, the dark cloth matching that of the regular human guardi, bore a small spiral crossed through with a single line.

Mell met them at the foot of the steps. "Finn." If there was a hint of relief in his voice, he ignored it.

The guardi captain nodded. Of a height with Mell, the man was built thicker, similar to Dub and Shar. "Mell. It is glad I am to see you, though I could wish it not be under such circumstances." His expression hardened, and he turned to his team. "Ward the alley. We need more than a general concealment. Keep everyone out. Then check it over. I want *everything* gathered."

As his men spread out, Finn knelt by Dano, one knee on the ground and his other foot propped on the bottom step. He ran his hand over the body, not quite touching. He, like Mell, had power in the spirit and emotion aspects, though his ran more to sensing any lingering energy signatures rather than direct emotions. Even if he had not met the person, or being, he could get an idea of who they were. He was also one of the best trackers of the guardi, and of the de Danann.

"You touched him." Finn's voice didn't change, but Mell could sense the disapproval.

Mell held his silence and Finn sighed. "I sense you and your brothers. There is a fourth, recent." He closed his eyes and inhaled. "She is in your kitchen. And, she is... not from here." The last was murmured in a soft growl.

"Eh. Don't you be getting any ideas there." Possessiveness moved through Mell. She was theirs; they'd found her first. She'd come to *them*.

Finn breathed in again and held it. Finally, he exhaled and opened his eyes, fixing his gaze on Mell. "There was another, but the trace is muddied, and possibly obscured by glamour." Then he added, sharply, "Is this fourth person the complication?"

Mell shrugged.

"She feels different. Like the Brigid, or even the..." His eyes widened. "You have a goddess in your home?" A grin spread across his face and he erupted into a booming laugh. One of the guardi spun around, eyeing the scene. Finn gestured, sending him back to his tasks.

"It is not that funny."

"The O'Loinsighs taking in a goddess? It is downright hilarious." He raised a brow, and his smile morphed into a smirk. "The O'Loinsighs, who have remained isolated in their little pub for the last century or so. The O'Loinsighs, who even before that have refused to take their place at their father's table and who have avoided the politics of the fae as though these were the things of Christian hell." Then the smirk fell away. "The O'Loinsighs who have a dead immortal on their doorstep. This, *she*, could royally fuck the balance of the area. We don't meddle with the gods. You *know* that. We serve them, or we avoid them. Damn, when you Fomoiri decide to shake things up, you go all the way."

Mell pouted, feeling like a scolded boy, something he hadn't been for centuries. "She's renting a room from us."

"And you didn't vet her?"

Mell shrugged and then checked on the other guardi, noting they were still a good distance away, though almost done with the wards. "Dub knew." He didn't think it necessary to explain further. Finn was a friend, but he wasn't family. Plus, it was the truth. Dub had at least suspected.

Shooting a glance at the closed door leading to the kitchen, and the goddess on the other side, he hesitated for only a moment before revealing the next piece of information. The guardi captain would find out soon enough. "She played the Dagda's harp last night. With Dano and I. We were having a bit of a sing-song and she just... picked it up and started plucking away."

Finn stilled. The whole alley, hell, the city, stilled with him. Or it seemed that way.

"The patrons enjoyed it. You'd expect protests or riots, or at the least a few thrown pints, but they simply... listened." Mell didn't know why the words were spilling out now. Maybe he needed to tell someone other than his brothers; maybe he just needed to get a reaction from Finn. "She's weak. From Dub's notes, her own people, even the other deities, have nearly abandoned her. She's... lonely. I think she just needs a place, a place to be."

"Where is she from?" Finn asked, his voice strained, and leaned back from the body he still knelt beside, the pose reminiscent of the ancient gestures of fealty.

Mell cleared his throat and looked away. This was the tricky part, the part none of the brothers had discussed yet. "Egypt."

"Fuck a lord's geese. Dammit, Mell." Finn blew out a breath. "What were you thinking, what was Dub

57

thinking?" He pushed to his feet, his movements sharp. "You have royally fucked the politics of our county, you know that?"

"Maybe, but probably not. As I said, she was all but abandoned by her people. And the gods don't really bother with us here in County Sligo."

"That was before someone played the Uaithne. An *Egyptian* goddess played the Uaithne. You know how territory hungry those bastards can be, despite how they fell out of favor. There are so *many* of them. Most of them are minor, and always looking for a way to increase their power. Cults are popping up all over the world. You *know* that." He shot Mell a disgusted look as he gestured for his men to help him gather the body. "Or, no, you don't. Because you refuse to enter the real world. You'd rather hide in your little backwater pub and diddle on your guitar."

Blood and adrenaline surged through Mell, and his hands curled into fists. Finn had gone too far. "Ye'r a bastard, Cumhaill, you know that?"

Finn shrugged, keeping one eye on his men as they picked up Dano. The left hand, the one with the ring, flopped out once again, as though asking someone to take what it held and get it to the person it was intended for.

Resentment and rebellion mixing in him, Mell descended the stairs, stopping on the last step so he looked down on the guardi captain. Barely a hand's span separated them. The other men paused, tensing, but Mell ignored them. "You just figure out what happened to Dano, and why someone is running around with a soul blade." He jabbed a finger into Finn's chest. "*We* will worry about the goddess." *Our goddess*, said a small voice from the back of his mind.

Finn rolled his eyes and Mell slipped the ring from Dano's slack grip and into his own pocket. Taking a half step back, Finn crossed his arms. "Right then. And what was Dano doing on your back stoop?"

Mell grinned mockingly and sent a thread of unease and anxiety at the other man, hoping to throw him off guard. "I have absolutely no idea."

The emotion was blocked and thrown back at him. *Damn protection runes*. He'd forgotten all guardi were equipped. Finn turned on his heel and stalked away, taking his men and the body with him. He was almost to the mouth of the alley when Mell called out. "You'll keep me updated?"

Raising a hand, Finn flipped him off. When they reached the end of the alley, the guardi disappeared.

Mell grinned. Yeah, Finn would be back.

He stepped off the last step and strode to the middle of the alley, opening his senses. With the last of his power reserve, he filtered through the emotions that lingered. He quickly dismissed the guardi, the trace of their feelings too fresh. Stalking toward the mouth of the alley, he paused when a track caught his eye.

A hoofprint, cloven, like a deer's, or maybe a sheep's. He pulled out his phone and snapped a picture. Not many sheep roamed the streets of Sligo proper.

He turned and strode for their back door, the door that would lead to his goddess and his brothers. He patted the pocket where the ring lay. Time to sort this out.

Chapter Seven

Bastie,

The Idiot's Guide is not a good reference. This was another of your jokes, wasn't it? No matter, I am learning so much of this land from the brothers. There is a grumpy one, a happy one, and one who is a little shy despite his size and the eye patch. Maybe they are like that child's tale we ran across?

- Bat, the confused goddess.

BAT

*B*at sipped her tea. It really was lovely. She could feel the care that Shar had put into it. It warmed her with more than the heat of the liquid.

"I should tell you what I saw." She glanced down at the crack Dub had left in the wooden top of the island. "But first I believe Dub should take a chill pill before any more damage is done to your belongings. I have a feeling there are many things about this situation that will cause an emotional reaction, and it would be best if we remained calm for the most part."

A choking sound came from the grumpy man beside her, and his shoulders shook. She set the mug down and twisted toward him. Laying a hand on his shoulder, she studied his expression, concerned. "Are you all right?"

Dub shook his head, but his shoulders jerked, and that strange sound still came from his chest. Plus, his face was turning red. Growing progressively more alarmed, Bat struck his back. Had he eaten something when she wasn't looking and then choked? She hit him again, but it didn't help. If anything, it grew worse.

She pulled back to strike once again, and a large hand caught her forearm. Shar grinned down at her. How did he move so quietly?

"He's not choking, *a stór*." Shar placed her hand in her lap but didn't draw his own away, leaving the warmth of his palm against her arm.

Bat looked more closely at Dub. His lips were pursed and twitched at the corners. His lapis eyes caught her gaze, and his shaking increased. Finally, he threw back his head and roared with laughter. "Ch- chill p- p- pill," he choked out.

She yanked her arm from Shar's grip and slapped Dub's shoulder. "It means you need to stay calm. Which you are utterly failing at." She tipped her head back and frowned up at Shar, who grinned down at her. "We should begin, yes?"

"Let's wait for Mell to join us, so you don't need to repeat anything."

It didn't take long. The back door swung open and Mell stepped through, his brows drawn together. He studied the scene—the laughing Dub, the grinning Shar— and his gaze lingered briefly on the new blemish on their furniture.

"Finn came." Mell shut the door and placed himself opposite her, across the island.

Dub sobered like a switch had been thrown. "Any trouble there?"

Mell glanced at Bat and then focused on his brother. "Maybe."

They were closing her out. Fair enough. She was an unknown goddess and, to a certain extent, invading their territory. But she would not be left out of the hunt for Dano's killer. The crime demanded justice, and she would see it was served. "Can I tell you of the visions now?"

"Visions?" Mell grabbed a strawberry and bit into it.

Bat eyed the bowl of fruit and pulled it closer. It was *hers*. She wasn't a selfish goddess, but... "It is polite to ask before taking another's food."

Mell stilled. Then, with a smile, he bowed his head to her. "I apologize, goddess."

She eyed him for a moment more and then nodded. "So, the visions. There was a dagger. It glowed with a dark light, one I am not familiar with. I think this is the reason Dano had to suffer the second death. We will need to find his killer and bring them to justice, or his ghost will haunt this place." She paused. Something was wrong with what she just said. She reexamined what she'd felt on the back stoop. "There was nothing of him left," she whispered. "Not even the ghost. How is that possible?"

"What else did you see in your visions?" Dub shifted away from her and turned so that he could face her fully. Avoiding her question?

Should she tell them all of what she saw, even the flashes not connected to the murder? If it had been Horus asking, she would have held her tongue. If it was Bastet, she would have teased with hints of new knowledge. When Isis used to seek her out, she knew to avoid mention of the attack and mutilation of Osiris, past or future. The goddess never wanted to hear it.

What would these not-men want to hear? And did she care?

"I saw a warrior at the prow of a ship, the wind whipping his hair, while his brothers stood behind him." She looked to Mell. "I saw Dano handing you something that glinted with gold, though I did not see what it was." She looked down and poked at one of the last two strawberries that remained in the bowl. "I saw two figures, one with green hair, one with red-gold, disappearing around a corner." She closed her eyes, reaching for the images. "The hand that held the knife was small. Pale and freckled. A woman's."

She paused. Dare she say the rest?

"That's it?" Mell ran a hand through his shaggy hair. "That's not much more than we already knew."

Her throat tightened, and disappointment swelled in her. So, here she was superfluous as well. No, she would not say the rest.

Arms came around her just as callus-tipped fingers

skimmed along the back of her hand. Apology and something like regret flowed from those fingers. "I did not mean you did not help, *realta*. I am simply frustrated."

"Ignore him. He is a right bastard sometimes, despite his charming ways." Shar's voice rumbled through her. The arms around her tightened, and he pressed his chest against her back. *Cuddling her?*

She drew strength from the offering of comfort and met Mell's gaze. Anger and defiance, the same that fueled her desire to leave Egypt—bolstered by the hope of home that Shar's arms gave her—allowed her to continue. "The girl with green hair. I met her. She said her name was Ailis, and she invited me to come to see her at O'Malley's."

"We know her." Dub leaned on the island, his hands clasped together. "Damn. That's just what we need, the trooping fae up in our business."

Mell shrugged. "They're in everyone's business. You know that. Though I wouldn't think her one to get involved with a soul blade."

More words that hung in her mind like riddles. Soul blades? Trooping Fae? The lack of a ghost, despite Dano suffering the second death. And what, exactly, *were* these men?

"But why was he here? I mean, at your place? He left last night. I saw you say goodbye." She leaned back, just a bit, enjoying the pressure of muscles against her back, even if they were covered with a thick sweater.

Mell's lips twitched as his gaze lifted above her and then shifted to Dub.

It was Shar who answered her question. "He made you the boots."

Her breath caught. Dano had made her boots? Her pretty, warm boots? Tears threatened and she swallowed. She lifted her right hand and enfolded her lapis pendant in her fingers. It was the last gift she had received, unsolicited, just out of the generosity of a believer. That was seventeen centuries ago. Now she had another.

She cleared her throat. "They are a fine gift. Worthy." Tilting her head, she furrowed her brows. "How did he get in? They were on this side of the kitchen door. It is why I thought you had left them for me."

All three brothers shrugged, including Shar. The movement rocked her, and the only thing that kept her on the stool was his embrace. "He was a leprechaun. It's what they do." Dub reached for her berries and she slapped his hand away. He gifted her with a twitch of his lips.

"Leprechaun. Huh. But not a god. And what are you?" She plucked up the second to last strawberry and held it up to Shar, her head tilted back to see his face.

The giant took it with a smile for her and a smirk for his brothers. "We are Fomoiri."

The name sounded familiar. "And Ailis? You mentioned trooping fae? Fairies, right? Is that why she has green hair?" She eyed the last strawberry then sighed. She *was* a generous goddess. She picked up the knife she'd used to spread butter on her bread and cut the berry in half. She held the first portion out to Mell.

He took it from her with a small burst of appreciation. "Ailis has green hair because she dyes it that color. And the trooping fae are... what we call the more gregarious of the sidhe."

"Shee?" She plucked up the last half and, hesitating only for a moment, offered it to Dub. See, she was a *very* generous goddess. She'd shared her strawberries, even with the crazy grumpy one.

"Sidhe." Dub took up the explanations as he took the fruit from her. "Another name for the de Danann. But, Fae can also be a general term for all the immortals." He bit into his piece of fruit and licked his lower lip.

She stared at that lip and her heart sped. Her belly clenched, and she crossed her arms over her middle, not because she was cold—how could she be with Shar's arm still around her?—but because she didn't know what to do with them. It had been how long since her last fertility rite? Other than the time with Seth and Horus, it had to have been at least before the uniting of the kingdoms.

Brows pinching together, Dub leaned toward her. "Are you having another vision?"

Heat bloomed on her cheeks. "No." She sat up straight, putting a few centimeters between her back and Shar. For a second she thought he would pull her back, but his arm dropped, and he took a half step back. She very deliberately avoided looking at Mell, for surely, he had sensed her moment of desire.

"Right... so, we need to find this soul blade, and then we will find the murderer, yes?" Had she read about a soul blade? And... Fomoiri? "Actually, I'd like to consult my Idiot's Guide. Bastet got it for me, and it has been a wonderful resource. It even talked about Sidhe and Fae, I just did not know that was how the words were pronounced." Eager to get her book guide, she slid off her stool.

"Idiot's Guide." Dub's eyes widened, and his shoulders jerked. He was laughing at her again.

Well, this time he could choke.

She nodded, firm. "Yes. It has many good things in it and has been extremely useful for figuring out your confusing culture. It even had a section on your holy man, the Saint Patrick. I quite like him. Now, if you... cretins will excuse me, I will fetch it from my room."

Chapter Eight

Bast,

They are curious creatures here. Did you know there are things called Immortals that are not truly immortal, nor are they gods? Like the griffon, but they are not animals. And there are so many kinds!

- Bat, the goddess who is a little less confused.

p.s. They keep giving me strawberries, and they are better than anything Hathor could hope to get her hands on.

BAT

By the time she returned to the kitchen, Bat had decided some things.

Yes, she was a visitor, but she was also a goddess. She didn't want to trespass, but she deserved answers. After she went through her guide, any questions *it* did not answer she would insist these brothers answer. They could argue it was none of her business. But it was. It *was* her business. Early in her existence, one of her many duties had been to help Ma'at maintain the balance against chaos.

And Dano had given her boots. He was now one of hers.

So, what was a forgotten goddess to do when she was presented with an opportunity to embrace a role once again?

She decided who she would be and then reinvented herself.

So many aspects from which to choose; so many different roles she had played through history. They were all part of her.

What did she want to be now?

She would be the balance. For her small slice of the world, she would push back the threat of chaos, and she would bring order and justice. Even if it was just for a small man, a leprechaun, who should not have died.

Because even if only for a few hours, he had been one of hers.

Bat paused at the doorway and drew in a breath, ready to demand the brothers stop being secretive and fill her in fully. Except there was no one in the kitchen.

They abandoned me? The old hurt tried to creep in and she shoved it aside. Not the time. *Never* the time, now. She was leaving all those doubts behind. Bastet said she had a complex about abandonment. Well, maybe she did have whatever that was—Bastet couldn't really define it well—

but now Bat was starting anew. *I just have to keep reminding myself of that.*

She stepped fully into the kitchen. Movement beyond the window over the sink caught her attention.

All three of them were out in the garden. Shar bent over the strawberry bush and plucked more berries. And... did she just see the bush wave at him? It was hard to sense, the earth aspects more often reserved for the gods, but the plant seemed happy to give him its fruits.

Heh. I'd give him my fruits. She snorted. Now she was channeling Bastet. The fact was, she'd give any of them her... fruits.

She shook off the errant thoughts. Maybe when she was done delivering justice to a murderer...

Dub stood at the end of the garden closest to the alley, arms crossed, once again frowning. He looked a bit like Seth. Not his features, he was much more handsome, but he had that same general dissatisfaction. *Unlike* Seth, he had shown her another side, one with humor, even if it had been at her expense.

Mell was in the far corner, the one she couldn't quite see but had wanted to inspect. If she craned her head, she could just make out the edge of his bent over form as he worked. "Dub, you could always come help," he said.

"No." Dub held his arms closer to his middle, causing the muscles to bunch under his sweater.

"You're not going to break them." Mell bent over farther, and she lost sight of him.

Dub shrugged.

"It was only the once." Mell's voice grew muffled, though she could still hear it just fine.

"Leave him alone. If he doesn't want to work in the garden that's fine. In fact, he's actually respecting my territory." Shar plucked another berry, examined it and nodded, placing it in the small basket he held.

"Unlike me, you mean."

"I did not ask either of you to come out here with me." The words were calmly stated, but a new tension entered his tone.

The garden was Shar's? It should have been surprising, but it... wasn't. The big not-man had a nurturing soul. *Fomoiri*. She gripped her idiot's guide, and though she wanted to open it and look for references, something kept her attention on the scene outside.

"We wanted to help." Mell's cheerful tones seemed amiss.

"And neither of you are."

Mell straightened, and she could just see the edge of his shoulder and the tangle of his messy hair. "I'm helping. See?" He held out a small bundle of roses, the new blooms a mix of pink and red.

Shar twisted toward him and frowned. "I wouldn't pick those. They shouldn't be blooming right now."

"Got pixies in the garden?"

"Don't call them that, you know they don't like it. And, I don't know what I have. Which is why you need to leave the bush alone until I can figure it out." The larger brother turned back to the strawberries and ran his hand over the leaves. They definitely waved back that time.

"They're another offering." Dub's voice cut through the air, and the plants trembled. His frown turned into a scowl, and he took a half step back. "Like the boots. Damn locals are giving offerings to the new goddess."

They were? They liked her? Dano's gift was understandable. They had played music together. But the others... She needed to find out who this other being was, this pixie. If they were to be one of hers, then she needed to know them. A smile spread across her face.

She hadn't come here looking for believers, but she wouldn't turn them away either.

Mell spun to face Dub. "You don't know that." A thread of fear, quickly squashed, leaked from him.

"It seems obvious to me." Dub's voice deepened to a growl.

Shar wove his way through the planting beds, touching a plant here, another there, until they seemed to glow with green and health. He paused by Dub. "We'll get it sorted." Then he called out, "Mell, get you and those bedamned flowers out of my garden."

Bat pulled away from the window, her cheeks heating, and hurried to her seat at the island. She busied herself opening the guide and turning to the index. It was silly to be embarrassed about listening in on them, but for some reason, she didn't want them to know she watched. The kitchen door opened and the brothers trooped in, filling the space and overwhelming her for a moment with their presence.

"I got it." She held up the guide with a bright smile. They all paused in unison, held like statues for a bare second, then silently continued to whatever tasks they had assigned themselves. Dub went into the pub area and returned with two more stools. Shar went to the sink and ran the new berries under water. Mell grabbed a glass vase from the top shelf of the open cupboard and placed the flowers inside. Dub went to fetch one more stool, returning just as Shar set a newly filled bowl of fruit in front of her while Mell set the flowers in the middle of the island.

"For you." Dub's deep tones sounded in her ear as he sat beside her.

Bat reached for a strawberry, and if her hand trembled just the slightest, she ignored it. "Thank you."

"You are welcome." His hand snaked over her arm, and he snatched her idiot's guide from in front of her. "Now, let's see what we've got here."

She bit her bottom lip as he flipped through the book with its bright orange cover, his mouth twitching occasionally. Shar nudged the bowl of berries, reminding her to eat, and she nibbled on the one she held.

Mell started humming under his breath, a fast tune, but somehow sad, like so much of the music here was.

"I didn't see anything on Fomoiri in there." She wanted to break this silence and get on with finding Dano's killer. How were they so calm about this? "Or soul blades. But, I just checked the index, there may be more buried inside, especially in the little bubbles."

Dub closed the book and set it before her. "I don't think you're going to find what you need in there. It's mostly speculation, and they have a lot of the history mixed up."

"He's still bitter about the whole Cu Chulainn thing," Mell said.

"Cu... Chulainn? Is this another of the words where

74

the pronunciation does not match the spelling? What happened with him?" she asked, once again sidetracked.

"Other than the fact that he's a lying braggart and made off with Dub's intended then didn't even marry her? Not much." Mell spread his arms wide and gestured grandly. "Per the history books we were raiders come to steal her as tribute, and he slew us in a mighty battle."

Bat stared at him for a full five seconds. "Does any of this have to do with Dano?"

Mell dropped his hands and shrugged. "Maybe. But I doubt it. Cuchi doesn't come around here often."

"We need to find the killer." She shot a glare at Mell. "Then we can discuss your weird names and confusing history." She tapped the island top with her fingers. "So, what is a soul blade, and why are the pieces of Dano's soul gone?"

Mell took a seat on one of the stools across from her. "Please, allow me to be your idiot's guide to the fae side of Ireland."

Dub snorted. "Well, the idiot part is right."

"Hush, you *cancrach*." Mell turned back to Bat as Shar grinned. "He's a grump, ignore him. I am perfectly capable of being your guide."

Bat tilted her head. "If you will take the place of my book, then can you please explain a soul blade to me? And... everything else that could help with Dano. The rest can wait. Though, maybe also why you are afraid that someone has made offerings to me. But first, the soul blade."

Mell sobered and nodded. He glanced at his brothers

then focused on the island top. "A soul blade is the only way an immortal can be killed."

Bat frowned. There was that term immortal once again. Maybe she didn't understand yet. "A god or goddess cannot be killed. Not truly. Therefore, they are immortal. Even Osiris, with all the fuss that was made, was simply moving into the next role of his existence, he was not actually killed. That the process was more brutal than he liked, well…" She shrugged.

In a way, she understood the human's need to use the terminology of death and afterlife. It was a way to bring comfort to their end, to make the stories familiar and relatable. Of course, then the pharaohs began appropriating the rituals for themselves… But the people had eventually reclaimed them, if in an overly complicated and bizarre manner.

"He was not killed," she said again. "Dano was, and thus he is not an immortal god."

"Ahhh. An immortal, not a god," Mell clarified.

She sighed. He was saying these were not the same thing. "But, if Dano was killed, then he is *not* immortal. Your terminology needs work." But this was also not something important to the current hunt for a murderer, only for her understanding of the situation.

"Yes."

Bat waited for him to continue. When he didn't, she offered him a berry.

He took it from her with a small smile. "A bribe?"

She shrugged. "You stopped talking."

"So, you gave me a berry."

"Yes, but it is one of *my* berries, so it should be an adequate offering for you to tell me more."

Dub let out a low sound that she couldn't quite interpret and Shar frowned. "Does everything come down to sacrifices and offerings and bribes for you?"

"Most of the time, yes, of course. I do not understand why this upsets you?" She looked between Shar and Dub, trying to interpret their expressions. She reached out to sense their feelings, but they were murky and confused.

"And... back to soul blades." Mell pulled her attention back to him. "At least here in Ireland, and through most of the Celtic lands, those who are not gods, who do not derive their power from believers, are termed immortals. We have powers as well and do not die of age, illness, or injury, but our powers are finite, neither growing nor shrinking with belief. And we can be killed, but it takes a soul blade." He drew in a breath and looked to Dub.

Bat turned her head to the not-man beside her. This... immortal. She had thought the only immortals were gods. Because in Egypt, they were. Even the Sphinx was a goddess, though a minor one.

She searched her memory. "Like... the griffon?" There were some creatures, considered monsters, who had made their way to her land from other countries and continents. The griffon was one such creature, and they had settled nicely in her home. They did not die, either, though they were more animal—or pet—than thinking beings. She'd only heard of one dying, in a battle a millennium ago, at the hands of a god wielding a dark blade... *Ohhh.*

"That can be one example." Mell bit into the berry and chewed slowly, licking a drop of juice from his lower lip.

"Hmmm... the griffon does not die from age. Neither does the Aani." She could count on her fingers the number of Egyptian "immortals" that were not gods, and every single one of them was a creature. It was something to think upon. "So, Dano was like the griffon?"

Mell chuckled. "He would have liked that. Dano, the mighty war beast of the sands, slaying the enemies of his goddess."

"And back to the explanations or we will be here all day," Dub cut in. "Most soul blades operate by absorbing the essence of the person they are used on. It is a very old form of sacrifice and worship that has fallen into disfavor. The blades are owned and guarded over by the gods. Or, our gods. We try to stay out of the politics of it. I do not know how they are crafted, nor do I care to."

"So, a god killed Dano?" It would fit with what she had heard of the griffon. "How will we narrow it down?" How many gods did they have here exactly? "Wait. The guide, it talked about the de Danann, it said they were considered gods. And some of the fae as well, and... We should make a list." She braced her palms against the island, ready to run up to her room for pen and paper, when Dub laid a hand over hers, keeping her where she was.

"Again, the guide was written by idiots. There are only a few true gods in Ireland, and most don't spend much time here, preferring their fancy homes in England and Germany. The rest of us, including the damned de Danann, are immortals."

"Well, that narrows the list considerably."

"No, you're not following. A *lann de anam* can be wielded by anyone."

Horror filled her. "It could be anyone…"

"I did find this in his hand." Mell reached into his pocket and pulled out a small ring.

It was an intriguing design. Two hands, clasping a heart with a crown. It looked familiar. "It's a claddagh. I know this one, it is a marriage ring." She turned to Dub and raised a brow. "I read it in my book."

Dub matched her raised brow and turned to his brother. "Does Finn know about this?" He didn't wait for an answer. "So, we have a secret love interest, unless Dano told you something?"

Mell shook his head. "There was also this." He pulled up an image on his phone and laid it on the table.

It looked like a print of some kind. Similar to an antelope, or even a barbary. "Your livestock roams in the city?" She didn't recall seeing any yesterday, but maybe that was simply because they were kept away for the celebrations?

"Not livestock. That," Dub said as he jabbed a finger at the phone, "is a gods damned baobhan sith. What in the hells is a Scottish fae doing in Sligo?"

"What is a Bevo—"

"Baobhan sith," Mell corrected. "It's a female immortal that subsists on the blood, and life, of men who long for their loves."

"And it should not be in our town." Shar finally sat, taking his place beside Mell. He picked up the phone and examined the photo. "I am not as familiar with them, but Dub would know. He's hunted them before."

Something like horror tightened her belly and threatened to send back up the berries. "You have hunted other immortals? Given them the second death?" *For isn't that what the soul blade did?*

He grunted. "No. We just track them down and send them home, reporting them to the branch of the guardi who is supposed to monitor them. I've only ever killed one immortal, and it was not a little fairy woman, however bloodthirsty." Dub frowned again, and it was the scowl she had first seen, the one that closed him off from others. Not a line of inquiry to follow right now.

"So, we have two women, one green-haired and known, a ring, and a print. We know the person who wielded the knife was female, or had very delicate hands, and is freckled. We also can assume Dano was here to—" she broke off and swallowed. "He was here to bring me new boots." She frowned, sorting through possibilities and unknowns. "Was the murderer already here, or was Dano followed? Who would have known that Dano would come back here? And if they were already here, was Dano the original target? Or was it one of you? And, how does a hoofed, blood-drinking female factor in? I didn't see any bites, but maybe they were hidden? And, if she was the killer, why stab him?" Bat shook her head and slumped. She nudged a strawberry with her finger but didn't pick it up. "Too much we still don't know."

"There should be no 'we' about this. The guardi are the ones who handle this kind of thing." Mell sighed and rubbed his eyes. "I know the guy who is running the investigation. He's good. He'll get to the bottom of this, figure out who's responsible."

"But he does not know what I saw." Bat didn't want to let this go. "Or have the ring you took."

Mell kept his gaze on his fingers and began picking at a callus that was peeling on his middle left finger. "I could call him, pass along the information. It... would be for the best, I think."

Disappointment stole the strength from her limbs and sent chilling hurt through her middle, where it mixed with the sickening horror that hadn't faded. She looked away from them all, from the berries and the flowers. The boots on her feet were suddenly too tight.

What Mell said made sense. The locals would be more likely to see what was out of place—what didn't fit—and catch the murderer. She would simply be in the way. She didn't even know the simplest of things about this land. There was no reason for her to be hurt.

But emotions and reason were not often in agreement, and he managed to hit her in the exact place she was most sensitive. He rejected her help. He told her she was useless, that someone would be able to handle this better.

And what hurt the worst was he was probably right. Doubt crept through her, and she blinked back the tears that threatened.

When did I turn into such an... emotional being?

When the visions promised hope. Hope really was the curse some said it to be.

Dub slammed his hand onto the table, and the new crack spread. "Stop it."

The doubt evaporated, and she gasped in anger. Anger and doubt. So similar. They could make your stomach churn, and your thoughts fly away. They were disorienting and dangerous. But anger could give you strength, where doubt only took it away.

She glared at Mell. "That was a despicable thing to do." Her voice was low, almost soft. But if she didn't keep it low, it would come out as a scream. "You... are a *wanker*."

"Wanker's English, not Irish. You'll want to call me a bollix," Mell said. The words were playful, but his voice was flat.

Dub reached across the island and to his brother, slapping him behind the head. Bat looked at him and nodded. "Yes. Good. He deserves violence directed against him for that *stunt*."

Chapter Nine

DUB

*D*ub suppressed another laugh. This girl... No, not a girl, *goddess*. She just seemed so young sometimes, alternately thrilled and grieved by a pair of boots. At other times, she was remote, almost chilly, exactly as he thought a goddess should be. Then there was her language. So formal, but occasionally she would spout some nonsense like "chill pill" or "stunt." The mixture of old world and slang was charming. And frustrating.

How was he supposed to keep his distance?

Maybe he wouldn't.

Now she looked at him with those star-filled eyes, a hard, angry expression on her round face. Her cheeks were flushed, and her chest rose and fell with her anger. His blood surged in answer, and he hit his brother again, never taking his eyes off Bat.

Her lips twitched and then stretched into a wide grin as Mell cursed and moved out of reach. Dub thinned his lips to keep them from forming into an answering grin. He pushed the strawberries closer to her. "Eat the fruit Shar picked for you. You're hurting his feelings."

The playful words slipped out. He felt it within himself, a softening in his heart. It had been like steel for nearly two millennia, and this softening was for a goddess who considered strawberries a worthy offering and sought justice for a leprechaun.

He knew for a fact that the only reason the guardi cared was because of the use of a soul blade. It meant someone was maneuvering for power, and gods did not give up their power easily. If Dano had simply been attacked… well, what was the harm in injuring a leprechaun?

He suspected Bat would have sought justice even if Dano had merely gotten a stubbed toe. Whatever floorboard or loose stone had perpetrated the act would have been eliminated with swift retribution.

She picked up a berry and sent an apologetic glance to Shar. "Sorry."

His brother smiled at her, gently of course. "He's teasing ya. It is very hard to tell, isn't it?"

"Oh." Bat peeked up at him through her lashes and then back down, before finally facing him. "I have learned some of your frowns, but it is very hard to tell when you are acting playful. I am used to more smiles when that is the case. I will work on this." She gave him a short nod and continued. "But can you explain why your brother decided to be a wanker?"

"Told you. Proper term's bollix," Mell said.

"I will call you a wanker if I please. I like this word better."

Dub's lips twitched again, but he quickly got himself under control. "I suspect he is concerned for you."

"Really?" Her eyes lit up and she turned back to Mell. "You are worried for me? But then why do something so wicked as to make me doubt?"

Mell's lips parted, but he didn't speak. Remorse and dismay were writ clear on his features, though he held the emotional threads back.

Dub took pity on him, though his brother didn't deserve it, and continued his explanations. "He called in Finn Cumhaill to handle the investigation. Or, he asked Finn to handle it and Finn agreed and pulled some strings to ensure his team was assigned. And because of who Finn is, and his power, he now knows you, a foreign goddess, are here and involved in the death of a fae." Her mouth opened, probably with yet another question, and he held up a hand to stop her. "Finn's Tuatha, of the de Danann, but he's still a good man. The problem is, he will have to report your presence. And after last night there will be rumors flowing already."

Her face fell with dismay.

So expressive. He swallowed.

"Because Dano made boots for me?" She swung one of her legs, and his gaze was drawn down. She really was stuck on those boots. A seed of jealousy wormed into the soil of his soul and put out a root. *Fuck.* He did not need this.

"No." His voice came out harsh, but instead of

drawing away as he expected her to, she frowned, matching him. "No," he continued, evening out his tones. "Because you picked up the Dagda's ever-loving harp, and proceeded to enchant a room full of fae who are more known for their rebellious ways than for offering anything to a god or goddess, ever."

She let out a frustrated sound, half groan and half sigh. Her hand closed around that necklace of hers and she pulled on it, lightly. Her brows furrowed. "You may be right about the idiot's guide. It has left a lot out. There was no mention of a dagda or a harp." She let out a light groan and rubbed a hand over her face. "I should not have let the cat talk me into this. I don't care what the visions promised."

What visions were these now? Dub shifted on his stool and cleared his throat, wanting her attention back on him. "The Dagda is one of the de Danann gods. He's a bit of an arse, but then, most gods are."

Bat's eyes widened, and her mouth dropped open. Then she smiled, wide and joyous. The smiled stretched until she was laughing.

She laughed so hard he was afraid she would topple right off the stool. Dub held out a hand, ready to catch her. He also caught the thread of Mell's amusement and enjoyment. Even Shar grinned wide. Dub's own lips twitched and then stretched.

The woman before him filled the room with mirth and took them all with her.

Finally, her laughter died away, and she wiped her hand over her face. "Oh, yes. Yes, gods can be real arses. I like this one. This word. I will use it. It is almost as good as 'chill pill.' So simple. Arse." She giggled and nodded, the grin still wide on her face. After a moment it faded away and she sobered. "I admit I did not think how your local gods would feel about my visit, but I cannot imagine giving up the hunt for justice for such a paltry reason. What could they do to me?" She tilted her head, a gesture that was becoming very familiar to him. "As you said, a god cannot be killed. Not truly."

Disappointment moved through him. And there it was, the arrogance—and selfishness—that seemed endemic to all deities. *She really was like the others.* He latched onto the thought.

"*We* are not gods." The words ground out of him, and he pushed back from the island with a force that sent the stool tumbling from beneath him and the island screeching into Shar's side.

Mell's face fell, but he kept a tight leash on his powers, not leaking any of what he must be feeling because of that... *goddess's* words. The word felt ugly to him now.

Dub had seen that expression before, though, on the day his brother had returned home from the last war, the one the humans liked to call The Great War. There was nothing great about a war fought without honor, with weapons that killed from a distance while the enemy hid.

His hands curled into fists and a haze fell over his mind, bringing dark memories of his own. There were many, many such wars fought, all without honor. And most of them were because of callous and cruel gods.

"Dub." Shar's warning tone cleared some of the haze and Dub realized he had moved. He had gripped Bat, his fingers digging into the flesh of her upper arms even through the thick sweater she wore. He squeezed harder and knew he could break her. She was so diminished. His strength wove through him, settling in his fingers.

Her gaze met his, and there were the stars he'd been fascinated with before. Now, they made him sick.

She didn't struggle. Instead, she relaxed into him, softening her body. Her head tilted, and her hair brushed over the back of his hand. "I'm sorry." She licked her lower lip. "I am sorry for my heartless words. This time I was the wanker."

Dub broke. That was the only word for it. Groaning, he pulled her closer and bent down, seeking her lips with his. When he found them a fire ignited, hotter than the forges he used to smith weapons in. Her lips parted beneath his and he invaded. Like the Fomoiri of old, he took her invitation and plundered, stealing away with her. *Well, with this piece of her*.

Something between a cry and a groan came from deep in her chest, and she clutched at his sides. Needing her closer, he skimmed his hands down her arms, over her hips, and he gripped her thighs, pulling her up to him. Her arms went around his shoulders, and her fingers dug in.

All the time the kiss continued.

Her legs wrapped around him and he kneaded the softness of the flesh where her thighs met her ass. Her *arse*.

A chuckle, wholly unprepared for, escaped him. He pulled his head back from her and studied the slightly dazed look she wore, her lips parted and soft.

A throat cleared to his right. A finger poked his shoulder to the left.

And a knock sounded on the back door.

Fuck.

He eased Bat back to her feet and gave her *arse* one last squeeze. However, he was in no condition to answer the door. "I think one of you will need to handle whoever that is," he said to his brothers as he grabbed a corner of the island and pulled it back into place, avoiding looking at them. He moved to the far side and used it to disguise the state of his body. He should probably go into the pub, they were due to open soon, and there was still work to complete, but he didn't want to leave Bat until all of this was settled.

He did not appreciate the chaos she had made of his emotions and thoughts, but he also couldn't deny this was the most alive he'd felt in centuries.

His goddess still stood where he left her, eyes swirling and lips swollen. He suppressed the urge to kiss her again and, instead, left the shelter of his spot and pulled her back to her stool just as Mell answered the door.

Chapter Ten

Bastie,

I may not send this one. But… one of them is a very good kisser.

- Bat, the blushing and befuddled goddess.

BAT

*B*at was barely aware of Mell answering the door, or the low voices. Her mind, her body, her very spirit, was filled with the feel of Dub.

Could a goddess go into shock? Because she feared that was what had happened to her.

The kiss had been amazing. But beyond it, she sensed a deep pain, one that she yearned to heal.

And maybe this was another reason she was here. The

brothers were out of balance. Dub, torn with pain and violence and betrayal, but filled with such need.

Shar, Searbhan, the giant. He was gentle, and calm, and seemed to maintain the balance between his own brothers, but there was something under it all, a sense of inadequacy, and a need of another kind, one to... protect?

Then there was Mell. Laughing Mell, joyous Mell, teasing Mell, who used his power, and constructed emotions to hide his true self. What hid behind that mask? Who was he really? Did he even know?

The price of a long life, as she well knew, was the opportunity to accomplish much greatness, but to also suffer an unending pain, if it could not be healed.

She had two months here. It was not much time, but perhaps, once Dano's killer was found, she could help these brothers that brought her strawberries, and flowers, and kissed her senseless.

"It's for you." Mell crossed the room to her, concern pinching his brows together.

Bat sat up straighter on her stool. "Me?" She slid off the stool, took a step to the door and then hesitated. "Who is it? I don't know anyone, yet. Is it Ailis? She knows I'm here." She pressed her lips together, realizing she was rambling.

"No, it is not Ailis. It's the pooka."

Another new term. She tilted her head in inquiry.

"He... has something for you." The caution in Mell's voice warned her to step lightly.

"Is there something I should know?"

Mell opened his mouth then closed it. He shrugged his shoulder and raised his hands.

It was Shar who answered her. "Just do not promise anything. Two reasons. The pooka can be tricky. Well, trickier than many other fae. Also, if the gods learn you are answering the supplications of those who come to you, it could put us in an... interesting position." He shot a tense look at Dub then looked back at her. "Just tread carefully. As you said, you may not be able to die, but the gods of this area could make things very uncomfortable for you during your visit."

She crossed her arms over her middle, hugging herself. "And you do not want any of that to come back at you." Unbidden, her gaze moved to Dub.

When none of the brothers spoke, confirming or denying, she nodded. "I will be careful. Thank you for the warning."

Turning to the door, she pulled it open and stepped out on the stoop.

Before her, stood the man she had noted the night before, the one with the long beard and who smoked a pipe. He had also sung with them from his seat, his gravel baritone offering a lovely counterpoint to the harp's sweet tones.

"Hello."

Though he stood on the bottom step, his head was even with hers—he was that tall. He'd been shrouded in shadow most of the night, tucked in his corner, and she had not seen his build. He was tall, taller than Shar, but thin, as though a normal body was stretched and pulled into an almost unnatural length. His beard, grey as the clouds overhead, curled down his chest and his eyes were a dark well. If she looked long enough, she would see to the heart of him. Darkness lurked there, and she suspected this particular darkness was not one she wanted to see.

He dropped his gaze and held a leather pouch out to her. "In appreciation of the night's celebrations." He peeked up once and then looked back at the steps. "For the harp. When you play not in the pub."

Bat looked closer at the offering. Yes, the shape of it was right. And similar to her boots, bright blue curled over the top flap in swirls and stylized animals.

"I—" She extended a hand but stopped short, remembering the brothers' words. It went against her instinct to reject such an offering.

The pooka's shoulders hunched. "It is offered freely." His voice lowered to a growling whine, like a hound afraid of the hand of its master.

Sorrow moved through her. What were the gods of this area like that this not-man was afraid to give?

She took the leather case from him. "It is beautiful, a worthy offering." She hesitated. It did not feel right to not give something in return. Balance. That was what this city needed. Its balance was off, just as the brothers' was off. Stepping forward, she laid a hand on the pooka's shoulder and opened her mind's eye.

Flash. A woman, thin as he, under a full moon. Flat marshes surrounded her, and a low mountain rose behind her.

Not much. She sighed. "You will find her on a full moon, in a marsh under a low mountain."

The pooka's eyes shot to hers, wide. He scrambled back from her touch and into the alley. Then he stood straight, bowed to her, and bolted to the main street. His movements were smooth, his long limbs allowing him to stretch and reach like a horse across the red lands.

She'd have to confirm what a pooka was.

The door opened behind her. "I forgot to ask his name," she said to whichever brother this was.

"Liam." Mell stepped to her side. "You didn't—" He shifted on his feet. "You didn't give him anything, did you?"

A curl of resentment formed in her belly. "Nothing that he asked for." She would not lie, but what gave these men the right to question her? She was a goddess that... was renting their spare room. She sighed. "I did have a vision. I told him what I saw, how to find his love. He did not ask for it, and the gift was freely given."

He grunted. "Probably get away with it." He nudged her with his elbow, and she looked up to see a mischievous grin. "Not that I honestly care. And, here is something to keep in mind. Dub knew who you were, or he suspected, but he *still* rented you the room. Something in him wants you here, or you *wouldn't* be here, goddess or no. He would have simply denied your application." Mell wagged his brows. "I'm glad you're here."

Bat laughed. Mell hid behind his power, but there was still a side of him that genuinely enjoyed playing. She leaned into him. "I will tell you something as well. I am glad I am here too, despite these events."

He wrapped an arm around her and turned them both to the door. "Well, let's get to it, shall we, and find us a killer." He opened the door and said in a voice lowered to a loud whisper that carried to the other two brothers where they stood, heads together. "Ignore the grumpy one. He's crazy anyway. Has been for centuries."

The two brothers pulled apart, Dub glaring at Mell while Shar laughed.

Dub turned to her and the frown eased. "We have... conferred, and we would be grateful for your assistance in finding the person who killed Dano. Any help you can offer. No strings, no supplications, no formal offerings or rituals or any of that crap. Just... what you care to give. If the guardi has a problem with it, we'll deal with them."

This was exactly what she wanted, but the way he put it... *Just what you care to give.* The words zipped around in her mind, bouncing and careening like a drunken sand fox. When had she ever considered what she *cared* to give? Not once had such a sentiment been directed at her. Pleas, orders, and demands, yes. Duty and purpose and fate, yes. Offerings and sacrifice and endless obligation she was compelled to fulfill, and for the most part was glad to do so. But this was something different, and it fed her like nothing else. It was *choice*. She had made her own decision about her new role earlier when she went to fetch the Idiot's Guide. Now it was being *offered*.

She wondered if Dub had any idea how precious that gift was.

"Of course, I will help," she said, forcing the words through a throat tight with emotion. She couldn't resist a little dig at the grumpy brother. "Is that not what I have been trying to do?"

Dub raised a brow and crossed his arms, not giving an inch. "Tell me again what you saw."

Chapter Eleven

FINN CUMHAILL

"You and Brian get the evidence and impressions cataloged," Finn ordered Criedne, his lieutenant. "Have Auden examine the body, and see what Sean can get on that print."

Criedne inclined her head and spun on her heal, heading off after the rest of his team as they carried the leprechaun's body across a small yard shielded from human eyes. Their headquarters for the Connaught region were housed in a renovated warehouse situated in northern Sligo, and while the myths of iron being poisonous to the fae were just that—myths—the metal *did* interfere with many of the rune magics. They could not transport themselves, or the body, directly to the lab for analysis, thus the small yard disguised as a delivery area.

There were many such things in his life now. Small adjustments that were made over the centuries to accommodate new technologies and ideas and customs, until the world he lived in barely resembled the one he'd lived in the time of mac Cormac. He missed that era, when there was no need to hide who or what he was, and a man could run screaming into battle on any given day.

Things were both simpler and much, much more complicated then. At least now the various Celtic deities had formed a sort of truce and worked together now rather than pitting their peoples against each other in battles none could truly win.

But, oh, some of those battles...

He, unlike the O'Loinsigh brothers and many of the other immortals, had never been anything other than a warrior, never wanted to be anything else. The Tribunal had declared after the Great War, that they would not sanction immortals fighting on behalf of or against human factions, unless those same factions sought to overthrow the gods' own rule and territories. As most conflicts since were more political or centered around the correct forms of worship for the Christian god, he hadn't seen a real battle since.

Not that the last war had been fought as a real battle. He could understand Mell's reluctance to face such a thing again. But being a member of the Ceilte Guardi was not the same as fighting in such a war. It was more the opposite, really. His job was to prevent the battles from occurring in the first place. And wasn't that a butt-kick for a warrior?

He pulled his thoughts from the past and took a

breath. They'd treat this as any other investigation. *He* would treat it as such. *But, a lann de anam.* Finn cursed even as his blood surged. He only knew of one soul blade not accounted for in the vaults kept by the Tribunal. It had been lost in a time he preferred never to remember...

And he would not. To dwell on such memories would serve no good purpose now. Setting off for the headquarters' entrance, he made a small detour, following a thin stone path to a stand of bushes. He offered a slight bow to the pixies housed there, ones who preferred to keep their smaller shapes and who were hired to guard the same entrance he headed for. They knew him, of course, but a smart captain maintained proper respect so as not to end dangling in the air from vines and roots and thorned branches that moved faster than he.

Branches waved toward him and leaves rustled. He bowed again, and finally headed inside. The warding ogham—*runes*, he corrected—glowed in a brief and faint pulse of welcome.

He headed straight for the captains' shared office. He trusted Criedne and the rest of his team to work through the details in the forensics labs.

The Ceilte Guardi had borrowed terms and techniques from the more modern police and human guardi, but they also possessed many that only those who could wield the forces of nature or manipulate the rune magics could do. Each member of his guardi could do both, to some extent.

There was no real need for a proper autopsy of the body, but Auden was a master at scanning for trace biologicals and imprints. While Finn could track those imprints, and gather a general sense of the person or being who had left them, Auden—given enough time and solitude—could tell you the last time that person brushed their teeth, or ate fish, or even farted. They would also be following the more human protocols of securing any non-biologic evidence left behind.

As their leader, he now had a much more difficult task to complete. He had to call a goddess. It was not something he relished. A situation always spiraled when one of the deities became involved. At least the Morrigan was easier to deal with than most, even if she became prickly over the strangest things.

Leaving behind the plain halls, he pushed through a pair of wood doors decorated in the spirals and knots of the Celts and entered his office. Well, his and four others. Fluorescent lights buzzed above and the harsh light they emitted blended with the cool daylight that filtered in through a bank of clerestory windows. The Captains' office was open to the warehouse ceiling, with the Chief's overlooking from the upper levels.

It was empty, the other units still out on their patrols. Connaught was a large province to keep under control with just four teams. He knew things were getting by them, especially since this particular province was where all the troublemakers seemed to want to settle.

He wasn't about to complain, though. No, he'd done that a few months before, and headquarters had transferred in a new unit. But whoever thought it would be a good idea to send farking Cuchulainn from Ulster to Connaught was an idiot. Immortals were, well, immortal, and they had *very* long memories.

Finn was not looking forward to the O'Loinsighs

finding out the other man was here. May have been dreading it even. Luckily, the chief had decided to set the newcomers to patrolling Galway, where there was a secondary headquarters for the southern edges of their territory.

Finn sighed as he sank into his chair. It was one of those modern contraptions that was supposed to perfectly support the body. It was very comfortable, but at the same time he couldn't help but wish it were plain wood or a plank bench. And that he sat with his men, drinking and singing along with a bard.

And these ridiculous longings and melancholy thoughts needed to cease. He knew why they were crowding in on him.

He straightened a few of the file folders sitting on a corner of his desk, then rearranged the order of the pens where they lay just above his blotter. He wiggled the mouse and woke his computer, then flicked a speck of dust from the edge of the heavy wood desk. Finally, he picked up the landline phone sitting at the corner and dialed a number all the guardi were supposed to memorize, though usually only the Chief dialed.

Finn hesitated and shot a look at the Chief's office. The lights were off. He really should report this and let Nuada handle it, but...

He groaned even as he punched in the number that would get him the Morrigan, the guardi's representative among the deities, and his patron goddess.

"This is Morri." The voice was light, with a slight sing-song.

Finn barely held back his snort. The voice she'd

adopted did not match the woman. Or goddess, as the case may be. "A leprechaun was killed last night on the steps of the Dubros." That should snap her out of whatever aspect she'd adopted for the day.

"Speak to me." Gone was the bouncy tone.

"That's what I know. There were some tracks, most likely—"

The line disconnected and moments later the Morrigan stood before his desk, brow raised. She wore black, of course, and had her lips and nails painted in red today.

Finn rose, hesitating just long enough to let her know he chose to do so, just as he chose to follow her.

"There is more." She crossed her arms over her chest, pushing her breasts together and up. Finn let his gaze drop in acknowledgment of her beauty, then gestured to the chair opposite him, inviting her to sit.

She shrugged. "I should not be here long."

Finn remained standing as well. "I suspect the tracks were made by a baobhan sith, but one of my team is verifying. The incident occurred sometime last night, late enough that the pubs were closed, even with the celebrations." He suppressed a smile at the goddess's quick frown. None of the Celtic deities appreciated their followers being stolen away. They had it easy, though, compared to some cultures. They were still remembered, and many of the customs had carried over to the new faith. The original gods of the area were plenty fed.

Not like the one he'd sensed at the pub.

"There is also a... complication." He did smile then, as he borrowed Mell's word. "A goddess is vacationing, and she is staying at the Dubros."

"Isn't that where Dagda decided to unload the harp?"

Sometimes the gods' and goddesses' disregard for each other astounded him. "Yes," was all he said.

She frowned. "She did not alert us to her arrival. I also did not feel anything, and I would have if a strange deity had come into my territory. Are you sure?"

"She is diminished to the point of near humanity."

"Then she should be no issue."

"She is from Egypt."

The Morrigan made no reaction to this, but that was almost as telling as if she had called for her ravens to pluck his eyes.

"As I said, she is diminished," he hurried to add.

A nod was all he received. The goddess's dark gaze drifted past him, and the lines of her face eased. After a minute, she focused on him once more. "Is that all?"

His reaction was harder to suppress this time. What did she mean, was this all? "Other than the fact that a lost soul blade has resurfaced, and is being used?" He narrowed his gaze. "Or has one been stolen recently? Is there something the guardi need to be made aware of?"

Her eyes narrowed in return, and she allowed a tendril of power to whip out at him.

The sting against his chest was nothing compared to the way fear suddenly stole the strength in his thighs, and he trembled against sinking into his seat. The Morrigan had once ridden into battlefields, bolstering her allies and taking the courage of her enemies. And she did it with entire armies. When even a portion of that was directed against one man, the effect was staggering. Literally.

"No," she said. "No, there have been no thefts. There

is only *one* blade missing from the collection. Of course, we may not know of all in existence. The Druids are tricky. But the knowledge of their creation has long been lost." She waved a hand in dismissal but didn't ease the pressure of her power. "*You* handle this one Finn. It's time you cleaned up this mess."

"We don't know it's them."

The Morrigan's power tightened further around him, and he struggled to pull in each breath. "You mean *her*." Then with a flick of her red-tipped fingers, she let him go. "I don't care either way. Just find the blade and finish it. I'll make my own decisions about our new visitor." Then she added, so low that Finn was unsure if he was supposed to hear her, "We don't need anything stirring up the fae in Connaught."

He couldn't disagree with her there. Connaught was where the Fir Bolg had retreated, and the Fomoiri after them, both troublesome races. It was where the solitary fae and the sluagh tended to gravitate. Hell, there was a pocket of goblins near Lough Beltra and a selkie pod off of Enniscrone that had a reputation for tipping boats and drowning fishermen.

The doors slammed open behind her and footsteps rushed toward them. He didn't take his gaze off the Morrigan.

"Finn, is it true that—" Oisin cut himself off. "My lady."

Finn could almost hear the bow the head of their research and analysis team gave to the goddess, though he didn't dare look away from her.

"Bard." The Morrigan turned to face the newcomer, and Finn allowed his attention to waver from the goddess.

Oisin stood there, red hair wild, clad in loose trousers and knobby sweater. The researchers weren't made to wear the uniforms, and in truth, Finn envied them at times. This particular researcher had a mobile clutched in his hand and averted gaze. "My lady," he said.

"Oh, come, poet. No need to be so formal." The Morrigan's voice took on a slightly coaxing tone. "Where are those words for which you are so famous?"

Oisin's shoulders hunched up and then, as though he had just reminded himself he was still the beloved of Niamh, the goddess of beauty, he relaxed and shot the Morrigan a charming smile. "Ah, forgive me, my lady. For I was overcome in your presence, as I always am."

She snorted. "Trite," she said, but with a quirk of her lips. "You had news?"

Oisin raised a brow and shot a look at Finn.

Finn nearly rolled his eyes, an action so loved by the youth of today. Did Oisin really expect him to instruct the researcher to not tell her whatever it was he had rushed in here for, when she stood *right there*? He made a give-me motion and Oisin nodded.

"She's played the Uaithne. I heard it from a pixie who heard it from the pooka. And the leprechaun was, apparently, up most the night making new boots for a guest of the O'Loinsighs who only had a pair of flats to her name and was shivering cold when she arrived." The last bit Oisin recited as though they were not his own words.

The Morrigan pulled in a breath then smiled. But it was not a smile that even attempted anything so benign as to convey joy or comfort. No, this was the smile of a battle goddess, and it sent both a thrill of anticipation and dread through Finn. A smile like that mean there would be blood in the future; his, the enemies, his family's. He could almost hear the cawing of the ravens and the clash of steel.

His blood surged and the strength that had left him only minutes ago returned in a rush. "Morrigan?"

"Oh, child. Oh." She shook her head, but the smile remained firmly in place.

Then she was gone, as quickly as she had come.

He focused on Oisin. "Get me everything you can on the Uaithne and this goddess. Everything."

"What about the blade?"

Finn strode from behind his desk. He'd told Morrigan what she needed to know. Regardless of where the soul blade had come from, there was a killer out there with it now. But that last smile... that was the kind of smile that heralded death for more than a leprechaun. He would need to know more of what was coming. They all would. "Put Midir on it," he told Oisin. "I have a feeling whatever is going on with the gods is going to be a little harder to suss out."

Oisin flashed an arrogant grin. "And I'm the best."

Finn gave him one that matched. "You are, son. You are."

Chapter Twelve

Bastie,

I keep meeting the most interesting people. Remind me to tell you more about Ailis. You two would get along wonderfully. She also likes to tease.

I am also having visions of a half-mountain the locals say is cursed. I almost squealed in excitement but managed to hold it in. Maybe they are not so unlike us after all, if they have curses.

I do wish you were here, though. These immortal not-men are confusing me.

- Bat, the goddess on the trail of a killer

p.s. Oh! I did not tell you! I am reinventing myself. I am going to become a disciple of Ma'at once more. I very much like the idea of seeking justice for those who have been wronged, and keeping the balance in a more direct manner.

I have always been jealous of the cat goddesses, who get to go hunting for the wicked.

BAT

They were here. O'Malley's, the first stop in their investigation. It was a mere fifteen-minute walk from the pub. This walk had been much different than the one the night before.

Celebrations and revelry for the saint were still underway. It seemed the peoples of this country could not decide on a proper ritual though. There were some, somber and respectful, nicely dressed and quietly going about their business; closed storefronts were the business equivalent. Then there were the others, in large green hats, or holding banners and ribbons, streaming in and out of pubs, or loudly singing, their accents so thick she wasn't sure they were speaking English.

The clouds parted, allowing a stream of light to illuminate the painted storefront sign of the shop they sought. It picked out the reds and deep browns in the letters and reflected off the glass, obscuring her vision for a moment.

When Bat blinked and focused, Ailis stood on the other side of the glass, a broad smile on her face.

The green haired woman yanked open the door and stepped back. "Ya came!" She gestured quickly. "Come in, come in. I don't have a lot of time, but I can fit in a chat." Her gaze moved beyond Bat to the brothers standing behind her. "Ya found the pub alright then?" She gestured again. "Come, come."

Bat entered the store and felt a pressure similar to the night before. Ailis's green eyes widened and shot back to the brothers as they came in, then settled back on Bat. "I had heard rumors, but..."

Bat noted that the accent, though still there, had cleared up considerably. She tilted her head. "Rumors?"

Ailis put on a wide smile. "Come into the back with me. Come on. We'll have a chat, and I'll tell ya of our little city. It's something, it's something."

Bat caught sight of an older couple in the aisles formed by shelves filled with various goods and foods. She nodded. "Yes, I would like that, thank you. And, thank you for the directions last night. Who knows how long I would have wandered in the cold. It was kind of you."

Ailis nodded, shot another closed look at the brothers and led the way through the little store. In addition to the aisles of goods, there was a low wood counter, weathered and old, just like the bar top at the pub. Shelves filled with jars and bottles were lined up behind it. An old-fashioned register, the kind with lever-buttons and numbers that flipped over, had a place of importance at one end. Bat wanted to examine it, and the scrolling metalwork that decorated its sides. Something of it called to her...

Dub nudged her back. "Don't be taken in by the glamour, *storeen*." Then he scowled at Ailis. "Tricky, tricky fae."

Ailis scowled back. "Not here, Fomoiri. Wait." Then she flipped her hair—and her middle finger—spun on her heel, and continued to the back of the store.

Bat laughed. Ailis reminded her of Bastet. She missed the cat. *I hope Ailis isn't the culprit. She would make a good friend.*

They entered a narrow room tucked behind the main store. A couple of small tables with chairs were crammed in there, and a narrow counter and sink took up space along one wall. A small plug-in kettle stood next to a box of tea bags.

Ailis moved right to it. "Care for some tea? How do you like it? Have a seat." She looked over her shoulder at Bat, brows raised.

She was supposed to answer now? Bat suppressed a grin. "Yes, tea would be lovely, thank you. I am not sure how he made it, but Shar put together a wonderful concoction earlier. And, yes, I would like to discuss something with you. Da—" Her throat closed. "Dano."

Ailis stiffened, and the mug she pulled from a cabinet fell into the sink. "Dammit," she muttered. She pulled out the pieces and placed them on the counter. The handle had broken off. She quickly pulled out another mug and filled the kettle, hitting the toggle to start it. She grabbed a second mug, and then two bags of tea, fussing until everything was ready for the hot water. When that was done, she slowly placed her hands on the edge of the counter and leaned into it, her head bowed. Then she spun and pinned an angry look on Mell.

"What did you get him mixed up in?" Her gaze bounced from brother to brother and she must have sensed what happened, or her abilities ran to reading thoughts, or emotions, or both. Her lids closed, and her face twisted. "What the hell am I going to tell Ciara?"

"The pixie?" Dub asked, his voice almost gentle. He pulled out a chair and nudged Bat until she sat. He took the one next to her, and his brothers leaned against the wall behind them. They filled the small space to bursting.

"Aye. She and Dano had an... understanding."

Mell shifted, and Bat knew he was going to reveal the ring. She wasn't sure it was the best move if Ailis was guilty, but it would be very smart if she was not. Reaching between her and Dub, he placed the small piece of gold onto the table.

Ailis sucked in a breath as her hand moved to cover her mouth. Tears glimmered in her eyes, making them look like the fields that covered this island. If she was presenting a false front, she was doing a very good job of it. Bat couldn't sense any traces of emotion from her. A trick of the fae?

"It's real," Mell murmured, so low Bat almost didn't catch his words.

Ailis pushed away from the counter and snapped up the ring. She turned it in her fingers, and once more her eyes slid closed. Her brow furrowed, and Bat could see her eyes moving beneath her lids. She slumped again and looked at Dub. "Not one of yours?"

"No."

One of his? Why would he have a claddagh, or, more than one? The confusion must have shown because Ailis grinned at her. "No, he doesn't keep a supply of claddagh on hand, ready to propose to every fae or goddess that steps into his pub. He's a smith." She snorted. "Used to be one of the best. Now he just does it as a 'hobby.'" The fae even held up her hands and made quote marks with her fingers. Bat grinned. Bastet used to do that too.

"We think there was a baobhan sith involved," Mell said.

Ailis paled. The kettle went off and she jumped, then busied herself pouring steaming water into the mugs she'd set out.

"Ailis." Bat didn't use any power, didn't seek a vision. Yet the other woman still flinched. "Dano was given a final death. A... soul blade killed him. And a woman with a pale freckled hand dealt the blow." Bat's gaze dropped to the other woman's hands, pale, yes, but with ragged nails and peeling green polish. Time for the doozy. No reason to hold back. "I saw you. You and another woman with red-gold hair, you ran from an alley."

Ailis's face closed up and Bat's stomach clenched. Maybe she shouldn't have been quite so blunt.

"And you want to know if I, or the woman with red-gold hair, had anything to do with Dano's death?" Her eyes narrowed. "And how the hells did you see this? I know when this was, it was months ago." She waved her hand and just like that she was back to the Ailis that Bat had met on the street the night before. "Eh, no matter. That was Ciara and me. We were spying on Dano. He was acting real shifty. We followed him to the alley behind the pub and saw him and Mell doing some sort of deal. Dub was there as well. And tell me, now, who does back alley deals with shifty Fomoiri? Shifty leprechauns, that's who. And that's what I told Ciara, she needed to drop him. But she refused and now look where she is." Her eyes filled, and she blinked. "And look where Dano is. So, tell me, what were you all doing in that alley, eh?"

It was a good question. Bat wanted to know the answer as well. She craned her neck back and looked at Mell expectantly.

Mell's eyes were wide, and his gaze bounced around the room.

Dub let out a frustrated breath and scrubbed his hand over his head. "Tell them."

"He was helping find Da's brooch." Mell's voice was guarded. He hunched the shoulder closest to Shar, a small cringe away from his brother.

Shar moved, an aborted movement of his arms, like he would hit his brother, or embrace him. The scowl on his face had him looking so much like Dub at that moment, if it weren't for the patch, Bat might not have been able to tell the difference. "You're both idiots." His hands flew up and Mell flinched. "Fucking idiots, the both of ya. What good would that do? It'll change nothing." Shar dropped a hand and slammed his palm into the wall behind him, denting the plaster.

"Hey now, easy on the walls. I don't want to be replacing that." Ailis straightened her slumped posture and glared at him. She turned to Bat. "Do you ever feel like you started reading in the middle of a series, but can't find the first book?"

"Yes." Bat grinned at her, appreciating the moment of humor. "I often feel like this around these brothers." She sobered. "I *am* sorry about Dano. We played music together last night. He made me feel very welcome. If you think it allowable, I would like to meet this Ciara and offer my condolences. It has... come to my attention, the ways of death are a little different for the immortals here. Know that if I could have, I would have ensured the parts of his soul found rest in the otherworld."

Ailis bowed her head. "That is kind of you, goddess. I will pass on your sentiments."

The sudden respect threw her off. "Thank you. But, please continue to call me Bat. I am no goddess here. I am barely one at home."

Ailis's green eyes met hers, glinting through her lashes. "I appreciate the generosity of the use of your name." Then she grinned and shot a look at Dub, who sat close enough for Bat to feel the heat of him. "Though I could argue that there are some who think you a goddess in truth."

Heat rushed to her cheeks and Bat cleared her throat. "Yes. Well. Back to Dano."

"Of course. Though there's not much I can tell ya. I will ask around about a baobhan sith, but I'm not sure what use it will be. Unless she didn't get her intended victim, you know she's probably returned to her mountains. I doubt she's using the blade for her own sake, that's not where a baobhan sith gets her power."

"Where would she get the blade?" Bat asked. "Would a deity have given it to her? Why would they? What purpose could it possibly serve? How does it give power? Does it use the souls it gathers? How many are there? Can just anyone use the power?"

Ailis glared at the brothers. "You *boman*. Did you not explain anything to her?" She leaned forward and gathered Bat's hands in hers. Their eyes met, Ailis's green ones eager. Bat couldn't even guess what her own expression was, but her thoughts swirled. "The soul blades belong to the gods, yes, but that doesn't mean that some enterprising immortal will not steal one occasionally and try to... raise their position in this world." She shrugged. "Or it's some pissant god who's decided he wants a larger slice of the pie. I don't know how they were made, and as far as I know, not everyone can use them or use their power, I should say. Anyone can kill with them, which is why they are locked up."

"So, the sith can't use the power?"

"No."

"Then there is someone else behind it."

"Find the sith, and you'll find the string puller, more than likely. Or figure out what they are ultimately after and get there before them. Dano and a soul blade, doesn't add up. It could have been random, a simple gathering of power. It could have been revenge, or he could have gotten mixed up with the wrong crowd. But how would they know he was going to return to the pub?" Ailis shifted her gaze to Dub. "Or he was just in the wrong place at the wrong time, and he took the blade for someone else?"

Ignoring the innuendos, for now, Bat turned her hands under Ailis's and gripped the other woman's fingers. She was careful to keep her power to herself. "Will you help us? I would like to find justice for Dano."

Ailis beamed at her. There was no other word for the smile the green-haired woman gave her. "Oh, ye're gonna stir up all the trouble in this little place. All the trouble." She turned her head to Dub but didn't pull away from Bat's grip. "I assume the guardi has been called?"

Mell cleared his throat. "Yes, Finn is on it."

"Well, that's got to burn yer britches." Merriment rang in Ailis's voice and filled the room.

Oh, she was one of those, like Mell. Well then.

"I asked for him," Mell said.

Was that a pout? Bat wished everyone would sit at the table, or at least stand where she could see them, especially if they were going to be part of the discussion. Her neck was getting a crick.

Bat squeezed Ailis's hands until the woman looked back at her. "And we are once again in the middle of a scene where I have not read the beginning of the book, as you said." She took a deep breath and slowly released it. She hoped this worked, that her powers cooperated. "I would like to try something, if you agree. I can sometimes get vi—"

"No." Dub shifted next to her and grabbed her forearm to tug one of her hands away, enfolding it in his. "Do not." His tones were stone. He would not move on this.

She argued anyway. "But if it could help—"

"Not more than it would harm if word got out."

Mell pulled out one of the chairs at the other small table and turned it around to face her. He leaned forward and propped his elbows on his knees, his long, calloused fingers clasped in front of him. "Word is out. She told the pooka how to find his lost love."

"A— a pooka's lost love?" Ailis giggled and squeezed the hand she still held. "More like his next victim."

Bat stiffened and pulled away. "I would never."

Ailis shook her head. "Pooka's don't have loves." There was condescension there despite the woman's cheery tones.

"This one does." Bat's words hung in the air, and tension rose in the room.

Gaze bouncing between the four of them, Ailis licked her lips. "All right then, ya told the pooka of his love. Yeah, the pooka's love." Her lips pursed. "Will you tell me of my love, then? Is that yer power?" Her green eyes twinkled with suppressed merriment.

"No, I have vi—"

"Bat." Dub cut her off once again, and she rolled her eyes.

Ailis grinned. "Don't be having ruptions, now." She reached out and squeezed Bat's hand. "You do what you may or may not be able to do, and we'll just see if it helps," she said to Bat.

Bat smiled and closed her eyes. Opening her mind's eye, she reached. The vision came easily, almost eagerly.

Flash. A flat-topped mountain that curved like a jaw. Slopes covered in green and the sun shining down. Ailis on the plain beneath it, new flowers spouting around her in dots of deep pink. She held a knife, the same as in the earlier vision. Opposite her stood a woman with deep brown hair, clad in a green gown that flared out in a gust of wind. Hooves. The woman had cloven hooves.

"Benbulben." The word slipped from her lips in a whisper, and Ailis's fingers went slack.

Bat opened her eyes, echoes of the vision still playing in her mind.

"There're effing stars in yer eyes, you know that?" Ailis slipped her hand from Bat's grip.

Mell chuffed. "Yeah, she does that."

"It's kind of pretty," Shar said from his spot against the wall.

Bat blushed, she couldn't seem to help it around these brothers. "Does this Benbulben mean anything to you? I... think we will find your balboa siv there."

"Baobhan sith," four voices sounded together.

"Right. That. But..." her voice trailed off. She didn't want to involve Ailis anymore, but the vision showed her being there. Bat had never tried to defy the visions.

The image had also not shown her or the brothers. It didn't mean anything, really. Just a snap in time.

Decided, she continued, speaking directly to Ailis. "Please do not go there without us."

Ailis scoffed and crossed her arms. "Wasn't planning on it. That place is cursed."

"Cursed? I know curses. Egyptians specialize in them, really." If this half mountain was cursed, it could explain what befell Dano. Curses were tricky, tricky things.

"Not literally, at least I don't think. But there always seems to be some tragedy happening there. The battle of the books and those squabbling saints. Or the thing with the deer." Her voice lowered. "Or the boar..." Ailis shot a cautious look at Dub.

"What was the thing with the deer? And a boar?"

"Nothing," Dub ground out.

"Dub put down a madman," Shar said at the same time.

Bat frowned. "You are all being very cryptic. Again."

She glared at Ailis. "Even you. I thought you would be better than these…" She gestured to the brothers. "Men." She injected her exasperation into that last word.

"Well, then let's lay all the secrets out there, shall we," Ailis said with a wicked smile and a wink. "Have you met Finn yet?"

The guy Mell asked to help with the investigation? "No, I was inside when he came." *And I have a feeling the guys don't want me to meet him,* Bat silently added.

"Well, Finn Cumhaill, leader of the Fianna, had some effing bad shit happen to him up at that damn mountain. More than once. And most of it was because of a bastard named Diarmuid. And Dub got sick of it and made sure it would never happen again. He became the boar."

The last part didn't make sense, but the rest certainly did. With dismay Bat turned to the man beside her, the heat he put off no longer warming her. "This was the man, the immortal, you… killed?" He'd mentioned it before, but, somehow, knowing the man's name made Dub's action real.

He stiffened, and she could feel him pull away from her, close himself up. But he didn't release her hand. "Do you believe in evil?" His voice was cold, hard, and she shivered.

Tugging on her hand, she answered. "Of course. If there is good, then there is evil. One cannot, by definition, exist without the other. And I have seen it."

"Well, sometimes the evil has to be stopped." He released her.

Suddenly she didn't want him to let her go. Her hand hovered in the air for a moment and then she rested it on his wrist, over a swirling tattoo that looked a bit like a hound. She didn't say anything, for she didn't know what to say. Maybe he was a defender of the balance, but she couldn't quite conceive of condemning a man to a final death in such a way.

But you did not even know of these "immortals" before you came here, did you? You didn't even know this was a thing, an option.

And what did they do with evil in her own homeland? They tried to right the wrongs done, and confine it through laws and teachings, keeping the evil and wicked gods' powers down. What did they do when that didn't work? The lionesses went hunting and restored balance. But they hunted the mortal, the humans who perpetuated the wrongs. And their souls were judged, weighed, and if found lacking, they were devoured.

Were her own people any better? Just because the judgment happened after death instead of before? And what was worse, to send someone into oblivion, or condemn them to eternal restlessness with the second death?

She didn't have an answer. But as a protector of Ma'at —of balance and order—she sensed no true evil in this man.

With a groan, Ailis dropped her head to the table. "Fuck me like a duck. Ciara. Her farm's out near the Benbulben. Could be the sith followed Dano from there, or to her. If you're telling me to beware the area, could be as simple as… We need to get out there." She jumped up. "And look, I'm no' going alone."

The others all rose as Ailis busied herself ushering the

few customers out the door, promising them she'd be open again the next day. Bat's mind swirled with unanswered questions, but she followed the others' lead, for now.

With these new developments, she was growing ever more sure Dano had not been the intended target.

Chapter Thirteen

Bastet,
I might get a puppy. And I do not care if this makes
you mad.

- Bat, the goddess who got puppy kisses

BAT

The farm was lovely.

That was the only word for it. Lovely. Neat rows of plants she wasn't familiar with lined one field. Another, separated from the first by a low stone wall, held a small heard of sheep. A tidy garden, blooming even in this colder weather, spread out in front of the compact house.

As they climbed from Shar's truck, a giant hound came running from the far side of the field of sheep. It halted just out of reach and lowered its head, a low growl rumbling from its chest. None of the others reacted, just stood there patiently.

"Ummm, should we not do something about the hound?" Bat suppressed a shiver at the chilling sound it made. She may be a goddess, but it would still hurt to be torn to shreds by a monster hound.

Ailis waved a hand. "She's just warning us. Ciara will be here soon, and then we can introduce you properly. Fina here is a right proper guardian, aren't you pet?" Ailis's voice dropped into a croon and the monster cocked its head, though the growl never stopped.

"Ailis!"

A slight female with red-gold hair emerged from the small house. She wore a faded dress of light blue. Bat looked her over, noting the light movements, the way the woman seemed to dance across the yard toward them. As with Shar, the plants of her garden waved as she passed, and she paused to pat a few of them.

When she reached her hound, she placed a small hand on its head. "Good girl. We know them." The woman's gaze fell to Bat and she tilted her head. "Well, most of them. Who's this?"

The words were said casually, but there was a wary knowledge in the depths.

"This is Bat. She's... visiting from Egypt." Ailis stepped forward and folded Ciara in a hug. "I'm so glad you're okay."

The other woman embraced Ailis, and Bat noted there were no freckles on her hands. But her hair... it was the exact shade as the vision.

You know that already.

There was something off, though Bat couldn't figure out what it was. There was something... she scanned the surrounding area but didn't see anything out of place. Not that she knew what was strange for this area. And wouldn't the hound warn them of danger?

Speaking of which.

Bat stepped forward, out of the protective circle the men had formed. "Hello."

The hound, Fina, growled again and crouched, though she didn't make a true move to attack. Shar's hand wrapped around Bat's waist and pulled her back against him. The hound's head shifted, a slight movement, but Bat suspected the animal was now focused on the one-eyed giant. The growling increased, and the hound took a step forward.

The next few things happened all at once, and it took Bat a bit to sort it out.

Ciara cried out, "Fina, no!"

The hound leaped, but not at Bat.

Shar was yanked from her.

And a herd of puppies tumbled out of the house, racing toward them.

Bat spun to see Fina standing over a prone Mell. Shar was on his hands and knees beside his brother, eyes locked with the hound. Dub held a dagger—*where did that even come from?*—and the other women were laughing as puppies bounced around them, giving off little cries and growls, some imitating their mother, others trying to elicit a pet.

One pup, a golden color that matched the light of a

just risen sun, approached Bat. It alternated between growling and licking at her boots.

She gazed down at the small thing, unsure what to do. Should she pick it up? Give it a ball? Pet it? Run from it? Dogs were herders and hunters, and Bat was neither of those. She hadn't had many dealings with them, other than Anubis. But he was a god, not a dog.

Be honest with yourself. You want one.

The golden pup sat back on its haunches and whined, giving her a big-eyed look that melted her heart.

Forgetting everyone else, she sank to the ground, cross-legged and held out a hand to the creature, utterly entranced. A low growl had her yanking the hand back as Fina, the mother, nudged aside the pup and placed herself before Bat. Sitting as she was, the hound was taller.

"Fina," Ciara said, approaching from the right. "Sit."

The dog whined but sat. Ciara once again stood beside her hound, a hand on her head, and looked down at Bat. "I apologize. We don't get many strangers around here. And, Fina's been jumpy the last week or so." She paused, and her gaze shifted to Bat's boots. A smile curved her lips. "Ah, so ye're the one my Dano talked of. He called me last night, going on and on about a woman who waltzed into the pub and played the Dagda's harp on St. Paddy's. Welcome be, then, welcome be." She said another word to the hound and the dog relaxed, flopping its bulk down in front of Bat and giving her the same big-eyed look as the pup.

"Ye'r shameless, Fina. Shameless." Mell sat up and held a hand out to the dog, who ignored him.

The golden pup tumbled into Bat and crawled into her

lap. She laughed and stroked her hand over it. The fur was a mix of rough wire and soft down. Its pink tongue slipped out and swiped at her hand.

"He likes ya." Ciara sat on her other side.

"He's lovely. Does he have a name?"

"Not yet. Maybe you would like to name him?"

It was tempting. The animal snuggled in her lap like he was meant to be there. Bat took a breath and lifted the pup from her. "If you would invite us in, we need to speak with you."

Ciara's hazel eyes filled with dread. "It's about Dano."

It wasn't a question, but Bat nodded.

"I was afraid, when he didn't come by this morning, that something happened." She pushed to her feet and dusted off her shirts. "Well, then, come on in and tell me what that blasted Leprechaun has gotten himself into now." Her words were light, but Bat could hear the tension.

Mell rose as well and extended a hand to Bat. She allowed him to pull her up. The five of them trooped to the farmhouse, Fina and the pups crowding in with them.

The place was small, the kitchen separated from a living room that was mostly taken up by a large dining table. Bat took a seat at one end and the golden pup came right to her, looking at her with those big eyes.

"No," she whispered down to it. He whined up at her. "Fine." She bent and picked him up, setting him on her lap. "You be good, or I will put you back down." She tried for stern, but her voice came out as a low croon.

This was why she never got a puppy, she suspected. That, and Bastet would disown her.

She looked up to find all eyes on her, the brothers narrowed, Ailis amused, and Ciara with a soft look of affection. Though, this last was directed at the pup, not Bat.

"So." Bat cleared her throat. "Ummm." She looked to Dub, instinct guiding her. She was the goddess, but he was the unspoken leader of their merry little band. "About Dano..."

His face relaxed into something resembling understanding and he nodded. He turned to Ciara. "Dano's dead."

The color drained from Ciara's face and she swayed.

All right, next time look to Mell. Don't use Dub for the hard news.

Though hopefully there would be no next time.

Ailis slapped his shoulder, just as Bat wanted to do. "Did ya have to tell her like that?"

He glared at the green-haired woman, and it held none of the softness he was starting to show Bat. *Good*, a small part of her whispered. "None of you were telling her."

"No, it's all right, Ailis. It's—" Ciara broke off as a small cry escaped her. Her face screwed up in grief, and she bowed her head, her shoulders shaking softly. They allowed her her grief. After a minute she took a few deep breaths and lifted her head. Her eyes were red but clear. "Who was it?"

Silence once again fell in the room. Even the pups remained still and quiet.

"We... think it's a baobhan sith. There are indications of one in the area." Mell reached across the table toward the pixie and Bat could feel waves of comfort coming off him. "We found him this morning on the back stoop of the pub. We think he was caught when he brought the boots for Bat." He gave her a soft smile. "He did a good job on them. Some of his finest work."

Ciara nodded. "He said he wanted to give her something in return for a good night of music, and that all she had were some flimsy flats."

Reminded of her bad preparations for this land, Bat colored. "I was not aware of how damp your home could become," she grumbled. Then her blush deepened as she realized she sounded ungrateful. "But, I do love the boots, very much. I am sure I have never owned finer."

A chill swept over her. It felt like one of the restless, the ghosts of those who had suffered the second death, but fainter. The uneasiness that plagued her outside the house returned. She peered around the room, looking for the source of the feelings. Something...

None of the others were disturbed. Could they not feel it? It was a point of chaos, of evil.

The conversation continued around her. Ailis offering words of comfort, Mell handing her the claddagh he had found on Dano. Dub questioned her about Dano's recent activities, and if she knew of any recent doings around the Benbulben, if she'd seen anyone, any strangers. That got a shaky laugh from Ciara, for who wasn't a stranger these days, with the tourists coming round for the celebrations?

Only Shar remained silent. His brows furrowed as he watched Bat. "What's wrong?"

"I do not know. Something is off..."

Fina stood and growled at the window facing the back

fields. Bat twisted in her seat and tried to see out of it. That sense of wrongness grew.

Her golden bundle of cute growled a puppy growl and pushed up from her lap, his front paws on the table, his head also twisted to that window.

"They've been like this for the last week." Ciara pushed at Fina's shoulder as dread grew in Bat.

"We need to leave. This is wrong." Bat clutched the puppy and rose, moving for the front door. Whatever was out there was heading for them, and the closer it got, the more she could sense the chaos of it. Like the evil that opposed Ma'at, whatever this was wanted to tear the world apart.

When the others didn't follow her, she stopped just short of the door. "Please. We need to go. I can feel it." She shuddered, and the puppy whined. "Please. Just trust me on this. Please. Until we know what it is exactly. Until we know what will stop it."

Flash. Shar on the ground, the soul blade buried in his shoulder. He was not dead, but the blade glowed with a pale rose that dimmed to black light even as she watched.

She clawed at the handle of the door. "Now. We need to go now. Now, now, now." Her heart pounded, and she couldn't catch her breath. If he died a final death... No. No, no, no. Not the gentle giant who brought her strawberries and whiskey tea.

She yanked open the door and a sharp crack rang out.

At first, she didn't know what happened. But with that

crack, the sense of wrong diminished, moved away, until it faded to almost nothing. She relaxed.

Then she became aware of a burning in her shoulder. The puppy struggled in her arms and she sat down, letting it go.

But then she couldn't get up again. And her shoulder hurt worse and worse. Huh. She looked down to see a dark stain spreading across her sweater.

Well, that sucks monkey balls. She giggled. She had hoped she would have a chance to use that phrase. Monkey balls. Who would want to suck those?

"Bat?"

"Little goddess?"

"*Realta?*"

A face hovered over her. Did that mean she was on her back? And she was getting cold again. *Dammit.*

The last thing she saw was Mell, a soul-deep pain shining in a face drained of color. He mouthed words she couldn't hear.

Why was he so sad? Did one of the puppies get injured? It wasn't as if a goddess could die...

But she could apparently lose consciousness. Black crept across her vision.

Chapter Fourteen

She'd missed.

Cursing under her breath, she sped deeper into the tree line. Not that there was forest to speak of these days, those cursed humans having cleared much of it to plant their pitiful crops and raise their bleating sheep.

Yes, she'd missed. Oh, how wonderful it would have been to see the shock on that Ciara's face as the bullet shred the pup's body. She'd been thinking to get rid of the mother hound, but then that newcomer had appeared in the doorway, the golden pup in her arms and she'd never been one to pass up such a perfect opportunity.

No, she didn't hit her original target, but the expressions of panic and, yes, *pain*, on the brothers' faces were just as satisfying, if not more so.

Who was the woman? She wore the boots Laina said the leprechaun was delivering to the pub. Was this the person who had set the wards around the pub that kept Laina from her true mission? Surely it was not the brothers. Even Fomoiri wouldn't stoop so low as to use the druid methods—those *humans* who thought they could enforce their own rules onto the fae. It was ridiculous to her, always had been. Who would defer to someone that had no true power, no glamour, and needed to create artificially?

It was the weakness of the gods and goddesses she supposed, to be reliant upon the supplication of those... animals.

She pushed out a huff of frustration as she reached her temporary housing and waved her hand to dismiss the hiding glamour. Surveying the run-down cottage, she huffed again, this time in disgust. To think that she'd put up with centuries of solitude and confinement, not even daring to exercise her powers to their full extent, all in fear of being found by the hunters, only to see them fawning over some other female. It was enough to curdle her stomach.

And that she had to live in such a place... even the baobhan sith had better accommodations.

No matter. Her plan, one centuries in the making, was soon to come to fruition. She only had to endure this a few days more, a week at most. There were a few more souls to gather, and the ones she wanted the most were those of the O'Loinsighs, one in particular.

As she pushed open the door of the cottage, Laina glanced up from her seat near the hearth. Her brown hair was matted, her skin pale and drawn. Faun hooves peeked from beneath her ragged green skirts. The sith of Scotland were strange creatures. In the light of day they were near hideous, but at night, their beauty rivaled even hers.

"I'll handle the brothers from now on," she told Laina. Then, because she knew she needed the sith's help later, she added, "You've done well, but even the best have yet to bring them down. And I need you whole for what's to come." The words nearly stuck in her throat.

"Yes, my lady."

She nodded. Soon. Very soon she would be able to answer to another title.

~

FINN

Finn stared down at the leprechaun's body. Dano. He would call him by his name, show him what respect he could.

Auden had removed the bloodstained coat and shirt to reveal a single wound in the abdomen, maybe three centimeters in length. It was a neat stab, no tearing in the edges, and for a human may have eventually been fatal—certainly would have been before mundane medicine improved to the point of near magic. The skin had gone that pale shade of lavender that all corpses seemed to hold, no matter their race or the darkness of their flesh.

"Anything?" he asked.

Auden, who was scanning the area beside the leprechaun's head, dropped his hand and opened his eyes.

"Quite a bit. It was definitely a baobhan sith who wielded the blade. I'll need to meet her to verify identity, but I'll know her when I do." He hesitated, lips pursed, then sighed. "As for the visiting goddess, I was able to get quite a bit. She did play the Uaithne, but she played it for comfort, from what I can tell. The leprechaun... appreciated it. It's actually the strongest impression I've been able to pick up. He was excited, but more than that, he was... hopeful."

Was that a trace of the same emotion in the other Tuatha's voice? "Auden," he said in warning.

"Right, my lord. If we returned to the alley, I might be able to pinpoint any lingering traces of the sith. If they are strong enough, we could track her from there." The other man kept his face averted and his gaze down. "Did the Morrigan really visit earlier?"

And there was another trace of hope and longing. Finn studied him. He was a younger fae, born sometime in the last few centuries. He had not been here for the Invasions, had not fought the Fomoiri or the Fir Bolg, had not witnessed armies of sluagh swarm his fellows. Had never heard the Dagda play his harp and call them to battle, nor had he seen Lugh on a shining steed wielding the burning spear. He had not been alive for when the gods walked among them in truth. "She did." Finn wanted to offer the man more than that but did not know the words to say.

Sometimes he felt his age.

"Finn." Criedne stood in the entrance to the forensics lab. "There's been an incident near Benbulben."

He groaned. "Fucking Benbulben. What?"

"The visiting goddess was shot with a high-powered

rifle of some kind while visiting a pixie in the area, the one the leprechaun had an arrangement with. The brothers have taken her back to the inn, but… the fae are stirred up. No one has gotten too out of line, but the pixies are swarming." Criedne's dark eyes drilled into him, challenging him and asking what their next step should be in the same moment.

"They were investigating on their own, of course," he finally said.

"No doubt."

"Send the body back. Spread the word that the O'Loinsighs will be holding a wake tonight. That should distract everyone and keep them away from our investigation."

She raised a brow. "You really think that will keep them away?"

He grimaced. "For a day or so. But, no, I'll need to do something about them."

Criedne's eyes went wide as the Morrigan appeared beside him once more. Twice in one day? Was this about more than the soul blade?

"This is a good plan, captain," the goddess said. "And I will accompany you tonight. The Tribunal has appointed me to assess this new goddess. If she is one in truth, she should be recovered enough by tonight for me to do so." She sent a playful smile in Auden's direction, who stared with wide-eyed awe, and then she disappeared.

"That was…" the young Tuatha said.

"Yes." Finn faced Criedne. "Arrange it."

She gave a short bow. "Sir."

Finn spun on his heel and headed for his office. Only

then did he allow himself to wonder how the brothers had reacted to the goddess being injured, especially Mell. The man had shown a definite possessive protectiveness, more than what a landlord would show for a tenant, and certainly more than a Fomoiri would show for any deity, let alone an Egyptian one.

Chapter Fifteen

Bastet,

I do not have much time now, but these brothers… they are more and more intriguing.

- Bat, the goddess who got cuddles.

BAT

*B*at opened her eyes and blinked. *What happened to the farmhouse?* She blinked again. *Oh, yeah, the pain in my shoulder.* She shifted, finding herself under a fluffy blanket.

She blinked again, and the room came into focus. Light pink walls and blue trim. Her room at the pub. Good. A light sound greeted her. She turned her head on the pillow to find Dub slumped in a chair beside her bed, his mouth open and soft snores escaping.

He looked peaceful, even if there were dark circles under his eyes.

He should take better care of himself.

She pushed the cover down and immediately snatched it back up.

She was naked!

Those... scoundrels.

Not that she minded being naked, but she was usually awake when it happened. Well, if it happened. Ugh, yes, it had not happened in a very long time. She glared at the sleeping Dub. And should not have happened now.

Her shoulder, the one that had been injured, was wrapped in clean bandages. She felt down her body and noted she still wore underwear, and someone had slipped socks on her feet.

Okay then.

She probed at the bandage, and when there was no pain, she searched for the edges, wanting to examine the wound. She didn't know what had injured her, but anything that could make her lose consciousness like that had to have been bad.

"Stop that." Dub's rough voice came from over her, and she turned her head to find him standing at the side of the bed.

"Hi."

His lip twitched. "Hi." He studied her, his gaze intense, then nodded. "I'll get Shar in here to check the bandage." He took a step back and paused. "Mell is... not well. It would be good if he saw you were awake."

Why would he put it like that? She frowned at him. "Of course, Mell can come see me. And Shar. But my shoulder is fine now. See?" She sat up, careful to hold the covers to her chest, and wiggled her shoulders in a little shimmy.

Dub grunted and turned away, but not before she spotted the smile.

A moment later the door opened, and Shar poked his head around the edge. Mell's voice rose behind him, distressed, though she couldn't make out the words.

"Can I come in?" Shar scanned her with his eye.

"Of course. Dub said you'd check the bandage. But, I really am fine. I'm not sure what hit me, but I'm a goddess, not much is going to keep me down." She tilted her head, wanting to tease his somber expression away. "Actually, nothing is going to keep me down."

He rewarded her with a small smile that soon fell away. Mell's voice rose, and she could make out the words "shot" and "kill." A wave of panic and bone-deep grief hit her.

Her hands twisted in the comforter, knotting the fabric. *Was that Mell?*

Her gaze met Shar's, and she beckoned him into the room. "Hurry, hurry. Get this thing off me and then find me a shirt. Hurry."

Shar looked over his shoulder then slipped into the room, locking the door behind him. He removed the bandage and examined the wound. His big fingers skimmed over the skin of her shoulder. "Nothing."

She grinned at him. "Of course not. I told you. I am a goddess." She added an extra dash of exaggerated arrogance, and he pinched her.

"Mell needs to see you, but... I needed to be sure you

would be up for it. He didn't take it well, seeing you go down like that."

"What happened?"

"You mean before or after your panic attack?"

She glared at him, trying to imitate Dub's scowl. "It was not a panic attack. There was something out there."

He gripped her shoulder. "Yes, there was something out there. A sniper with a long-range rifle, by the looks of the wound." His voice deepened even as she felt a warmth flow into her, one that originated from his hand. "Next time you get one of those feelings, I would appreciate it if you would allow us to check it out, instead of opening a door to who knows what."

The warmth continued to permeate her body. A sharp pinch in her upper back and she sighed. She hadn't even noticed the pain from the bit of bone still out of place.

"And you just healed me." These not-men were full of surprises.

He shrugged. "It is secondary to my ability with plants. But, I have some skill with healing. Now, if you're in really bad shape, you'll want Finn. He could bring someone back from the brink of death with just a sip of water from his hands. I've seen him do it. It's something." He patted her shoulder and stood. A moment later he handed her a sweater and a pair of tights. "I'll give you a few minutes, and then I'll send in Mell."

"Why do you and Dub keep saying it as though sending him in would be like slipping an asp into my bedroom?"

Shar's shoulders hunched. "He just had a bad time with it is all."

"Shar." His name came out harsher than she intended, but she was tired of everyone being cryptic. That was the purview of the gods, damn it.

He wouldn't meet her eyes. "He fought in the Great War. A lot of us did. Not Dub, it was his turn to stay behind. But it was harder for Mell. These modern wars... they are not an easy thing for warriors of honor. When you can kill an enemy, who is hundreds of kilometers away, without ever having to look them in the eye..." He trailed off, eyes trained on the floor. He swallowed and finally looked up. Pain was writ clear on his face, his blue eye shining through a shimmer of tears. "War these days is not an easy thing for a man like Mell."

Or for a gentle giant. But Bat held that thought to herself. He didn't need that right now.

"Could you make me some of that tea? Ailis' was good, but yours is better."

He blinked then bowed to her, his braid falling over one shoulder. "Of course."

She nodded. A passage from the Idiot's Guide came to mind. It had said that you should not say thank you to the fae. It seemed a silly thing to her—and had she not been saying it for the last two days?—but she would try to abide by it. Of course, if the brothers were to be believed, the guide was probably wrong. She wondered if there was any truth to iron being poisonous to the fae, and four-leafed clover driving away evil. These would be very easy measures to take...

Shar left her and she rose, hurrying to wash her face, brush her teeth and put on her clothes. She had just emerged from the bathroom when her door flew open and Mell stood there.

His hair and eyes were wild, his face pale. He gripped the knob as he stared at the empty bed.

"Mell."

His head twisted toward her so quickly she heard his neck pop. Their gazes locked, and she crossed to him. She took his hand from the knob and gently closed the door. She didn't lock it, though she was tempted to. She didn't want the brothers interrupting this.

She reached up and cradled his cheek in her palm. "Mell," she whispered. "May I?" She wasn't sure exactly what she asked permission for, but when he nodded, she acted.

One hand still on his cheek, she reached up to his shoulder with the other and pulled him down until she could reach his mouth with her own.

The kiss she gave him was light, gentle. She opened her mind's eye, calling for the visions, even as dread filled her. She didn't want to see whatever they would show her, whatever had put that look in his eyes and clouded his mind and emotions in sorrow. She didn't want to see it, but she needed to, to help share his burden.

She molded her lips to his just as the first one hit her.

Flash. Moans of pain and the tang of blood blended with the stench of rot. A young man's face, barely out of his youth, with wide brown eyes clouded in death. A boot-clad foot, but no leg. A scream of machines and the explosion of bombs. Death. Everywhere death and more death, and no one to properly lay them to rest.

Everywhere such pointless death.

She pulled back and went onto her toes, placing her lips against his forehead, bestowing what blessing she could. If she were more powerful, she could have taken him into her and wiped these memories away—could have restored the balance in his soul.

But she was not. And for the first time, she regretted that for more than just her own sake.

"I am sorry that this has happened to you, and to those men. I wish I could take your pain." Her words were soft, but they seemed to echo in the room.

He pulled away from her and his eyes slid closed. A sound escaped him, a soft sob. That was it. That was all he would let out. The grief still pounded through him.

"Would you like to come lay with me?"

He let out a choking laugh and his head fell forward. "I don't think I'd be of much use to you right now, though I appreciate the proposition."

She resisted the urge to hit him for half a second. Then her fist met his chest and he jerked, his head shooting up and his eyes meeting hers once more. Surprise replaced some of the grief. "No, you wanker, I meant to... cuddle. I have read that it is soothing for some and can help with grief."

He grinned at her, his mask back in place, and snaked an arm around her middle. "Well, then, yes, let's... cuddle."

She huffed. "That is off the table now." She moved out of his reach and to the window, looking out at the canal, though there was not really much to see from this angle.

"Bat," he said, his voice soft. "I would very much enjoy a cuddle right now."

She stiffened and turned back to him.

The mocking cheer was gone, and in its place was a tired man. She didn't feel the sorrow anymore; he must have locked that back away. Relenting, she held out her hand to him. When he took it, she led him to the bed and lay down. He climbed in behind her and wrapped an arm around her middle, pulling her back into him.

She fit very nicely. Like she was meant to be there.

His brothers never bothered them. They lay in silence for so long Bat wondered if Mell had fallen asleep. Then his hand lifted. He smoothed it down her side till it came to rest against her hip. "I was so scared," he whispered. "I could see you, silhouetted against the door. The sun shone behind you, and you glowed, like life and laughter and everything good. You were frantic, and I needed to get to you." His fingers dug into her, and she reached back until her own hand found his hip. It was a little awkward, but she needed to touch him, to reassure him somehow. "Then—" He broke off and she could hear him swallow, feel the movement against the back of her head. "Then the shot rang out, and I froze. I froze, *realta*. I couldn't—"

He shook. She resisted the urge to turn. Instead, she found the hand on her hip with her own, and pulled it around her, cradling it to her chest. She allowed him his grief.

Chapter Sixteen

Bastet,

I attended a wake tonight. It is a kind of death rite and much more fun than the ones performed in our land. I also met one of the goddesses of this land. She is as powerful as Isis, may even surpass Osiris or Horus in power.

And, she is feared by the immortals here. But I do not see evil in her. In fact, she reminded me a bit of Sekhmet. I think you would like her too.

I know I insisted I wanted to do this on my own, but maybe you could come for a visit?

- Bat, the goddess who misses you.

BAT

*B*at and Mell wrapped up another tune, this one an Egyptian funeral rite. Bat led on the harp and Mell accompanied her. Two other musicians, a banshee by the name of Meera, and the pooka of the other day, Liam, started up another. This one about some man named Finnegan and dancing with a sheet. Or was Finnegan in the sheet? She didn't understand most of the words, but it had her foot tapping, and definitely invited her to dance, with a sheet or otherwise.

She set the harp against the back wall, where she had found it that first night, and where it was when she entered the pub this night.

When she and Mell had finally come down from her room, the pub had been full. Dub had gone ahead and unlocked the doors to the fae customers when he saw she was all right, and the patrons had poured in.

The whole night had quickly turned into an impromptu wake for Dano. Bat's understanding was that this was a party to celebrate the deceased. It was very different from the death rites she was used to, but as there was no spirit to care for, she guessed it made no difference.

"Bat." Ciara stood before her, her red-gold hair bound back, and her face drawn. "I wanted to make sure you knew I had no idea anyone was out there. The dogs... well, they have been acting up, but I could never find anything amiss."

Bat smiled at the pixie. She believed her. "I know. But, could you let Dub or one of the others know when the dogs act up again? If whoever that was has been lurking for a week, they will likely be back."

Ciara shook her head. "Eh, no. I can't stay there if someone is lurking like that. If that's Dano's killer, they may come after me next. I'm going to stay with a... relative."

Another fae she meant. Bat nodded. "I wish you luck." Another thought came to her. "Do you know anything of what he was helping Mell with?"

The pixie shook her head. "Only that he was successful. Mell was supposed to fulfill his end of the bargain in two days. I don't know what the payment was, though. Dano liked to be secretive about his deals. He called them his pet projects and was very protective." She smiled softly. "He was a stubborn man, that leprechaun."

"I am glad I knew him, even for such a short time." They were the only words Bat could offer, but she meant them.

Ciara nodded and moved on through the room, talking and laughing.

Bat walked over to the bar and watched as Dub served customer after customer. Sometimes he would fill a pint glass with the dark brown beer favored in this area; sometimes it was the golden liquid, whiskey, that made Shar's tea so good. And, sometimes it was plain water.

A body stumbled into her, and the foul scent of stale tobacco and day-old liquor invaded her nose. She moved back from the figure and her eyes met ones that glowed red. The man grinned at her, revealing sharp teeth.

She smiled back, baring her teeth as well. They weren't nearly as sharp, but she had some skills.

"So, ye're the goddess who plays the precious harp, are ye?"

The man's breath was even worse than his general body odor, and Bat waved a hand in front of her nose. "I do believe I am."

The man leaned in closer, and Bat resisted the urge to back away. She would not give ground to this disgusting thing. "Will ye play a tune fer me if I give ye a sweet reward?"

"Neall." Dub speared the man with a sharp look. "Back off. She'll not be making any deals with ya."

The foul man, Neall, shrugged and wandered to the other end of the bar, skimming over the crowd with his red eyes.

Dub tapped the bar, pulling her gaze back to him. "Careful with this lot. They like to make deals, and ye're a visiting goddess who may not know the rules."

"I think the rules of supplication and rewards are the same in all places."

He raised a brow. "Not for the fae, little goddess. Just watch yerself." He moved back down the bar and pulled another pint, placing it in front of a small man who had a bit of the look of Dano. Another leprechaun?

She eased up onto a stool and surveyed the room. It was a good night. She enjoyed the laughter and song, all in tribute for a man they had once known and was now gone.

She decided this was a practice her own people should adopt. She would tell...

The front door clicked open. *Wasn't that supposed to be locked...?*

A darkness flowed through the pub, obscuring her sight of what stood on the threshold. Bat reached out, but it wasn't a... bad darkness. It was actually quite soothing, like the end of the day, when it was time to lay down to rest, or the end of a life well lived. Bat smiled into the darkness and greeted it.

"Do not even presume to greet me thus in my own land." A cold voice sliced through the darkness, disbursing it.

The woman who stood there towered over most of the men, standing as tall as Dub, still behind the bar. In fact, the only one taller was Shar. Bat's gaze drifted to where the giant stood against the wall, frozen in place. She sought out Dub and then Mell. Both stood still as stone. A quick survey of their patrons yielded the same results. *What...?*

Then she saw that their chests still moved, fingers twitched, and eyes darted. They were simply frozen in... a tendril of emotion reached her from Mell: fear, caution and a warning.

But this goddess did not feel evil, not like the encounter from earlier. How could they be so frightened?

The new goddess glided through the crowd, and patrons scurried out of her way as she approached. She halted before Bat and flicked her head, sending the wild waves of her midnight hair flying over her shoulder in a cloud. Her pale skin stood out against the black of her coat and the blood red of her lips.

Bat's lips twitched. Some goddesses could be so... dramatic. This one reminded her of Isis, imperious and assured, but with a hidden warmth.

Then she spoke. "I am the Morrigan. And you have trespassed." The voice remained cold, but something, some wariness, underlay it.

Bat wondered if anyone else could hear it. She tilted her head and studied the woman before her. Regardless of all that, it was only proper to show respect to the deities of whatever land you were in. Bat slid from the stool and bowed. "I offer my apologies. That was not my intention. I simply desired a brief vacation from my duties in my own land." *Or the lack of them.*

The Morrigan must have heard, or known, because she snorted. "You have no duties in your own land. You are a diminished goddess, of no import."

And then Mell, that idiot, that *imbecile*, stepped between the two of them. "If she is so diminished, then she is no threat, now is she?"

"Mell," Dub growled out a warning as he moved down the bar toward them.

The Morrigan held up a hand, halting him. She looked Mell up and down. "I remember you. The son of Alatrom who is more de Danann than Fomoiri, and who my top captain wants to bring into the guardi." She lifted her hand in a graceful motion and ran one finger, the nail painted in a bright red to match her lips, down his chest. The movement should have been sensual, but all it held was a threat.

Bat stiffened, ready to step in, when the Morrigan flicked her finger and stepped back. "Brave, or possibly stupid. But fearlessly insane as all the Irish," she said as she looked again at Bat. "I was sent to assess this new goddess, but I see the worry was for naught." The eyes moved down to her feet and back up, and Bat felt small and unkempt next to her. Just as Isis always made her feel.

So, Bat did what she always did when the goddess deigned to acknowledge her. She killed her with kindness.

"Would you care to stay for a drink? We are having a small celebration for a friend. I believe you call it a wake? Shar could make you some tea. It is quite good." Bat widened her eyes and tilted her head again.

The Morrigan's eyes narrowed on the smaller woman and she snorted, shooting a look to Dub. "She speaks for you now?"

Ignoring that comment, Dub gestured to one of the stools. "You are more than welcome to stay for a bit. As she said, we are having a wake for Dano."

The goddess hesitated. "The leprechaun that was killed?" Something new entered her voice, a dangerous note that brought to mind battlefields and the cawing of crows. A thirst for blood, but not mindless, no. A thirst for justice.

Something they had in common.

Bat held out her hand. "Please do stay."

Chin lifting, the Morrigan nodded and turned to her guards. There were four of them ranged behind her. The tallest, with short reddish hair, glared at Mell.

"We will stay for a few songs. You are welcome to drink to the deceased, but do not become intoxicated." The Morrigan took the stool next to Bat and locked her eyes on Dub. "A whiskey."

Dub nodded and quickly fulfilled the order, saying nothing as he placed the short glass in front of the goddess. A fresh mug appeared before Bat, the tea steaming, and she smiled at Shar, who gave her a brief nod and then returned to his place against the wall.

They sipped at the same time, and the silence grew. The patrons remained quiet and the music silent.

"Not much of a wake." The goddess took another sip.

Bat, eased by the tea and the small bit of kinship she felt for this daunting woman, answered without thinking. "They are a bit intimidated."

The Morrigan twisted her head to stare at Bat, her face still, but with a twinkle in her dark eyes. "Yes, I believe they are." She spun on her stool and looked over the crowd as the patrons avoided her eyes. Releasing a quiet sigh, the Morrigan settled her gaze on the harp where it sat against the back wall, just as Bat had left it. "You play?"

Bat followed her gaze. Was that a trick question? If the Morrigan was here to inspect the new goddess, surely, she knew Bat had played the harp? Especially if this was a god's harp, as the brothers claimed. "Yes." She took another sip of tea.

"Will you play me something?"

The room held its breath. Mell and the red-haired guard stiffened and looked between the two goddesses. *Why was a request like this so significant?*

"Of course." Bat slid off her stool and moved to the harp, taking the seat that had become hers in the circle of musicians.

Her fingers played over the strings, a tune that had no direction, as she thought of what to play. Unbidden, the song from her first night here came to her, and she picked up the tune. Mell took his own seat, taking up the melody with his guitar. A pipe joined in a moment later, and then a fiddle. Bat sought the same sense she'd given the patrons just the night before, that of comfort and home. She wove it in the air and sent it toward the goddess who sat isolated and alone at the bar, a small gift, freely given. For weren't those always the best?

When the song was over, Bat's gaze met that of the Morrigan, who nodded, said a few words to Dub and then exited the pub. Three of the guards went with her, but one remained, the red-haired one. He stood in the corner against the front wall, arms crossed, watching the patrons.

Once the goddess was gone, the atmosphere of the pub lightened. Bat and Mell stayed with the musicians and played a few more songs. A short couple got up and danced, and occasional laughter rang through the room.

Life continued, despite those who were gone. It was this the Irish celebrated, and Bat embraced the sentiment, as different as it was from her own people's customs. Though, the ancient ways were mostly gone, weren't they? Supplanted by the waves of invaders who brought their own traditions and deities and beliefs.

She just wished Dano's spirit could have seen the care and celebration for himself.

At midnight, Dub started kicking people out. There were a few grumbles, but on the whole, everyone left without a fuss. A few lingered, one of them being Ciara, the other Ailis. They stood talking with the red-haired man and Bat eyed them.

The celebrations were over, the dead honored. Time to find out what was going on, and continue the hunt for a killer.

She gave the harp one last strum and rose, placing it in its spot. She'd have to bring down the case later, so it was there when she needed to use it. Of course, she still didn't know what the harp did, other than augment emotions. Maybe that was all it did.

She stalked to the bar, Mell close behind her, just as Dub closed and locked the front door. Shar also joined them, coming from the hall, probably from locking the back door.

"What was that all about?" Bat's voice rang through the room that suddenly felt too big.

Ciara's eyes widened, she leaned into Ailis and whispered something too low for Bat to hear, and then looked at Dub with wide eyes.

"Ciara needs to go, get settled into her new place. We'll sort this all out in a moment," Dub said with a look at the red-haired man.

"Bat, will you help me wash up behind the bar? The sooner we get done with this the sooner we can deal with our... visitor," Shar said, his deep voice guarded.

Who *was* this "visitor"?

She cast one more look at him then moved around the edge of the long bar and to Shar's side. He showed her what to do, which basins to use for cleaning and rinsing, and finally how to dry the glasses. He stood next to her, helping, as Mell cleared the tables. Bat caught sight of Ailis working as well, wiping down the tables. *So, she didn't leave with Ciara.*

The only one not working was the red-haired man. He stood in the same spot he had all night, arms crossed, watching. Bat could feel his gaze on her occasionally, measuring. The occasional tendril would poke at her mind, easily blocked. Unlike what she felt from Mell, this was harder, analytical, less of emotion and more of reason.

The fourth time the probing came, she grew tired of it and opened her mind, allowing the other in. Then, in a move she'd learned long ago and had had no reason to practice recently, she wrapped a bubble around that probe, locking the other's senses away. It was a children's game, something she had done with Horus when they were younger. It was also a test of strength, to see who could best the other.

Unfortunately, this red-haired man was currently stronger than her and ripped through her bubble like it wasn't there. She flinched, and a glass slipped from her fingers, shattering on the floor.

"Shit." Shar picked her up and set her on the bar. "Are you okay?"

It was unnecessary, Bat wore her boots, but she enjoyed the care he took. "I'm fine." She laid a hand on his shoulder, assuring him. "I was just distracted for a moment." She resisted the urge to glare at the red-haired man.

"Yeah, Finn here decided he'd mess with the goddess, see what reaction he could get." Mell hopped up on the bar next to her.

A snort from the redhead. Finn? The man they spoke of earlier? "She started it. That was a neat trick by the way."

She twisted so she could see him fully and pinned him with a knowing look. "And you deserved it, poking at me like that."

Mell and Ailis chuckled as Finn's eyes widened. Shar's shoulders shook, and even Dub let out a low bark of laughter.

"Believe me, goddess of Egypt, you will know when I poke you."

Bat glared at him even as the blood rushed to her cheeks. *Arrogant not-man*. He was almost as bad at the brothers, but *much* less endearing.

"Should we not get on with this?" Bat held her arms out to Shar. The big man gifted her with a small smile and plucked her up by her sides. He walked with her held out from him like a messy baby and set her down by one of the tables dotted through the room. She gave a soft laugh and patted his shoulder. "Thank you." Then she twisted and glared at the others in the room. "Everyone, come sit."

No, she may not have much power left, but she was still a goddess of balance and a guardian of order against chaos. That gave her some leverage here. She assumed this man was here to discuss justice for Dano, and that was her area of responsibility now.

Pulling out a chair, she gave them one last glare and then sat.

And, of course, they obeyed.

She looked at Finn, who sat across from her, and waited. The corner of his mouth ticked up and he flicked a quick glance at Mell before once more settling his gaze on hers. His own were a soft hazel, more gold than brown or green, and glowed softly.

Not a weak man.

"The Morrigan has agreed to allow your presence in

her land on some conditions," Finn started. Dub shifted forward in his seat and opened his mouth, and Finn held up a hand, stopping him. "She came here tonight to assess you. It is always worrying when a new deity comes in, especially if they have not first made contact with the local deities. Most know to do this." He let the words hang there.

What was she supposed to say? "I blame it on the cat. She helped me plan."

"Excuse me?"

"Bastet. She helped me make arrangements. It's the kind of thing she would do, leave out a detail like contacting the local deities, or telling me I should, just to see what happened." Bat shrugged, not really concerned.

"Alright, yes, we can... blame it on the cat. Now, on to the conditions. You may not set up a place of worship." He held up his hand again, forestalling protests. "Meaning, you may not answer the sacrifices of those who come to you. The Morrigan will allow offerings freely given, or," his gaze flicked toward where the harp rested, "the use of any artifacts that call to you, as well as small supplications. She understands a goddess must have something to sustain her and was not best pleased with your state of... deterioration."

So, the boots and the harp case would be allowed.

The glow in his eyes grew. "She also wanted to let you know the song was lovely, and a worthy offering in itself."

Bat pressed her lips together. She had not meant it as an *offering* to the Morrigan, simply a... yes, it was an offering was it not? But not from a supplicant to a goddess, simply a gift. Finn remained silent, waiting for a reply.

"I am glad she enjoyed the song." There, that was neutral enough.

His lips ticked up at the corner again, and he nodded. "I will relay your words." He drew in a breath and anticipation filled Bat. Finally, they would get to what mattered. "As you know, Mell asked me to head up the investigation into Dano's murder."

Bat nodded, the others following soon after her.

Finn pursed his lips. "He probably thought I would share information more easily than others."

Disappointment spread through Bat, and she gripped her hands together. He didn't sound as if he planned to share anything.

His head tilted, and the lamplight glinted off his light red hair. "He was, of course, correct. On one condition."

Dub growled. "No more conditions."

Finn leaned back in his chair. "I am afraid I cannot be lenient with this one. There have been signs of a baobhan sith in the area, as I am sure you are aware of as well, since the print was found in your alley. I also know you went to a farm near Benbulben this afternoon, a pixie's farm, and that you left in rather a hurry, with one of you injured. I know that pixie was here tonight and that she was involved with Dano. And I know Dano was helping you find something, asking all over creation about a brooch." Finn shook his head. "Why would you ever ask a leprechaun to find something for you? That's like asking a wisp to lead you through the forest, or a pooka to give you a ride. Asking for trouble it is."

"He found it." Mell's quiet tones were filled with something that might have been sorrow, or anticipation, or even resentment. There was too much there for her to sort through.

"And what did he find for you?"

"Mell," Dub said.

"No, there's no reason to keep it a secret. He found me Da's brooch." Mell leaned his forearms on the edge of the table, and his shoulders slumped.

"Ye'r a damned fool, Mell O'Loinsigh." Finn's whisper, thick with brogue, had Mell slumping even farther.

"I know."

Bat's gaze bounced between the two of them. She remembered the conversation from earlier and Shar's reaction to the news. She looked now at the pain shown in Mell's posture, a pain older and much different from what haunted him earlier.

"Does any of this have to do with Dano's death or tracking the killer?" she asked.

"I have no idea. We don't have much to go on, and we need to follow each thread. For all I know, the true killer is the pixie, and the baobhan sith was simply in that area." Finn's voice was cool, the brogue almost gone.

A tell to make note of.

Bat opened her mouth to protest the last statement, explain that they knew better, but a sharp movement of Dub's hand cut her off. He didn't want her to speak of the visions.

Her anger grew. So what if she spoke of them? She was here for two months. Maybe she had vaguely hoped for longer, but she only had the room secured for two months. If she spoke of her visions and had to return home sooner, was that any worse than a delay in catching Dano's killer?

No.

"It wasn't the pixie. And it wasn't Mell, or any of the brothers." Finn's eyes widened as she spoke, and a smile played at the edges of his lips. "Nor is it Ailis."

The green haired woman, silent until now, crossed her arms and groused. "Bet your bullocks it's not me."

Bat continued, keeping her gaze locked on Finn. "Nor is it a red-haired wanker who came into a pub tonight and rudely stood like a statue through a celebration of life," she said pointedly.

"Then who is it, Bat of the two faces, who is rumored to see the past and the future in her visions?" Finn's body remained relaxed back in his chair, but an eager tension radiated off him. It almost made him handsome.

Also, hah! They already knew. So much for Dub's cautions.

Mell pushed up from the table. "Dammit, I knew that pooka was going to be a problem."

Finn shrugged. "Wasn't the pooka, though I heard about that too. The guardi has some resources, which you would have access to if you would just reconsider my offer."

"And we have gone off on another tangent." Bat understood much better now why Mell didn't want to join the guardi, and he didn't need this not-man constantly throwing it in his face. "As you said," she directed this to Finn, "I have visions. I know the shape and look of the hand that wielded it. It was a woman, and it was none of these people I have met." She didn't mention the vision of Ailis at Benbulben, unsure if that actually tied into their current situation, though it was likely. She also wasn't sure she trusted this red-haired man.

Bat opened her mind's eye, seeking answers, uncaring if she offended. At this point, either she would need to leave, or she would stay her allotted time.

Flash. Benbulben. A woman of amazing beauty, glowing in the sun, her red-gold hair a lovely complement to Finn's light red. They were beautiful together. An argument. A kiss and a slap.

Flash. This same woman, weeping over a still body, her face ravaged by grief and madness, her hands gripping her hair, tearing at it. The blade on the ground next to her.

Flash. Finn, his hands cupped, holding water as he stood in a familiar alley.

Bat came back to herself as Finn pushed away from the table and jumped to his feet.

"You dare," he said, glaring at her.

She raised one brow, intending to come out with some smart comeback, but instead, a question slipped out. "What happened to the woman?"

Finn froze, and his face turned to stone. "I will not speak of her."

It was interesting that he did not ask what woman. "Really? You are willing to prod Mell into something you know he does not want, yet you will not 'speak' of a woman, one I just saw kneeling next to the very same blade I also saw stabbing Dano? It glowed with a dark light and had a serpent's head on the pommel. What happened to it?"

Finn paced to the bar and spun, heading back to the table.

"What happened to the blade?" Bat asked again, keeping her voice gentle, needing him to speak. She almost had this. Almost had the answer, it was coming together...

"The blade was lost that night."

"And you kept that hidden from everyone," Dub broke in, but his voice was soft just as Bat's had been. He sounded as though he knew the night Finn spoke of.

Finn looked at him, something like regret in his face. "Yes. The Morrigan knows for I would not lie to her, but most think it was placed in the vaults. The panic..."

"Ye're a bastard." Ailis slapped her hand on the table. "Ye'r a right bollix who should be swallowed in a bog and spit back out ye're so sour. A soul blade, *lost*." She rose and paced across the room, muttering, just as Finn had done.

The Irish are sure a dramatic people. A glimmer of an idea reached her, seeped into her mind and grew. It was almost like a vision...

"We can track it."

Ailis spun around. "What do you mean?"

"I mean *I* can track it. I sensed something this afternoon, at the cottage. A point of—" she swallowed and shot a sneaking look at Dub. His bright blue gaze was trained on her. "A point of evil, of the chaos that threatens and must be held off by constant vigilance and order. That was what it felt like, and it moved. I could sense when it drew near, and when it faded with distance."

Dub met her gaze and gave her a slight nod. He had heard her. Good.

Then he spoke. "It would be best if you stayed out of it from this point."

"Excuse me?" Anger and hurt churned in her.

He looked first to Mell, then Shar, and his lips thinned. "I'd like you to let us deal with this. Finn can track the baobhan sith, once we get a starting point. If you were hurt..."

"I'm a goddess. Haven't we already established this?"

Shar gave her a pleading look. "But you're weak. A little blood loss had you out for the better part of five hours. And since the Morrigan put a ban on supplicants, you're not going to get much more power than you have now."

Then Finn jumped in. "I was able to break your hold on me very easily." He sounded speculative, though, not agreeing or disagreeing with Shar and Dub.

"But if she can track the blade and the bitch without needing a jump off, I think that's worth a little defiance. I could have dozens here by the morning with offerings..." Ailis spun around and resumed her pacing, muttering quietly to herself and pulling out her phone.

Bat looked to Mell, the only one who hadn't spoken. His face was pale, his brown eyes haunted. "I—"

Finn cut him off. "If she can track the blade, we will need her."

Bat gave this guardi, this red-headed man who—more than Dub—reminded her of Seth in the early years, a small smile. Then she reached for Mell's hand and gripped it. "Goddess, remember? I'll be fine." She looked at the brothers and remembered Dub's earlier concerns of what may come of he and his brothers. "If you'd rather not be involved, I understand. Finn and I can work on this." She ran a thumb over Mell's knuckles. "It is really all right. I would rather help in this small way than watch and do nothing. I have had too much of doing nothing."

"Eh, it wouldn't be just you and the arrogant oaf." Ailis dropped back into her seat. "I'm in. I called Meara as well. The banshee's in for some light surveillance and will spread the word to others who can keep an eye out for the bitch, though yer likely to only see the sith at night." Ailis nudged Bat's leg with a foot. "Maybe the Morrigan doesn't want you here, but most don't mind a goddess who gives a shit."

"I think you do not give your Morrigan enough credit." Why Bat felt the need to defend the goddess she didn't know. She recalled the look she'd seen when the other goddess spoke of Dano's death. Whether it was for Dano, or the trespass of her authority, there was a part of the goddess that cared very much.

Ailis waved a hand in dismissal but didn't speak again. Bat caught her shooting wary looks at the guardi. She suspected if the man had not been here, Ailis would have been much more vocal.

Bat took a breath, avoiding the stony looks of the brothers. "So, where do we start?"

Chapter Seventeen

SEARBHAN

Shar clenched his fist under the table.

Release. Clench. Release.

The little fool was determined to get herself into trouble. Oh, the folly of protecting a goddess. She would always do what she willed.

And Finn had officially taken over their little conference.

Fucking Finn.

Shar shouldn't be so angry with the de Danann for holding back what he knew of the blade, and the most likely person to have taken it. After all, hadn't Shar himself fallen under Grainne's spell, even if only for a bit, in the Dubros woods? And hadn't he failed in his own duty to protect the Rowan? And wasn't he, even now, holding back by not speaking up?

Finn had failed in far grander, though less obvious, ways. He was the one who let Grainne and Diarmuid evade the hunters all those years. Oh, it wasn't obvious, and every time the couple slipped through his hands, there was a reasonable explanation. And when Dub had stabbed Diarmuid, Finn had delayed in his healing, not because he wanted justice for those slain, but because he feared that if the man lived, he would never gain the woman.

But Shar had seen Finn's expression as he avoided each mention of that woman tonight. There was anger and pain, but there was also a longing still. He wasn't fooling anyone. Grainne had had him on the road to twisted, and after all these centuries, he lingered with one foot on that dark path.

As Bat said, she was evil chaos. He wondered if what his goddess had sensed was not the blade, but the woman. Pure speculation on his part, as they had no confirmation that she was involved in this, only the snips of images that Bat received. They could be putting the pieces together in all the wrong ways.

But someone had shot her at the pixie's farm, and Bat had sensed that something was amiss before the shot was taken.

Bat, Ailis, and Finn sat, heads bent together, and made plans. Shar wanted to snatch his little goddess back and pack her into her room.

Then he remembered the look in her eye when Dub had told her to stay out of it. The anger, and yes, hurt, that clouded her starry gaze. It had only grown when Shar spoke, backing his brother up.

No matter what she thought, and what Dub implied, they were not worried for their own safety. They were concerned for hers. And, yes, for Mell as well. Shar sometimes wondered if his brother might not wake one day and welcome death, decide to take that final step and fade to the Otherlands. He never did, he always found a reason to continue, but if anything happened to the little goddess... Mell had not reacted well to her injury.

Confusion churned inside Shar. He was not built for this emotional warfare. Despite his size, he was always more comfortable with his plants, and his wood. He shifted in his seat, drawing the eyes of his brothers. Bat kept her head averted, not looking at any of them.

It was a small loss and not one he was okay with.

He stood. "I'm going out to the garden."

His goddess turned her head to him and he caught a glimpse of her round features, closed and distant, as they had never been, not even at that first moment when she stood on their doorstep and Dub had been so rude to her.

Dub rose beside him, and Shar waved him away. "Please, no. I just need a moment to think."

Mell glanced up at him and then back down. His middle brother had a tight leash on his powers, and his emotions, at the moment.

She is a guest. Shar reminded himself of this. *No matter what she makes me feel, what she makes all of us feel, she is no more than a guest and will be gone soon.* Besides, what would happen if the brothers decided they did want her and did something about it? Dub's kiss earlier had been abrupt, but he would not have done it if he did not feel something. Mell's reaction to her being shot was very telling, and Shar himself had very much enjoyed the brief moments he had held her body to his. After just one day, even his thoughts were telling, filled with possession. He already thought of her as *his*.

Maybe he could gather some berries for the morning.

He made his way to the back hall and the small laundry where he kept many of his tools. Pulling down a small basket, he mused over what had him upset.

Is it really that she wants to be involved?

He strode through the kitchen and to the back door.

Is it that I want an excuse to protect her?

He pulled the door open and bounded down the steps, taking two at a time.

Is it that I fear how my brothers will react if she were harmed?

He opened the small gate and stepped among his plants, his babies, and sent a small tendril of his power snaking among the leaves and stems.

Is it that I fear how I will react if she were harmed?

His babies answered him, sending sleepy feelings of dark and contentment back at him.

Or is it that I know my brothers and I will never be the same now that we have met her, and we will break apart when she leaves?

He crossed the garden to the back corner where the berry bushes grew. He took his time, selecting only the best berries. They needed to be just this side of ripe. Too far and they would be over sweet. Not ripe enough and the tartness overwhelmed. A branch rustled, and he reached deeper, finding a perfect berry. "Thank you." He sent an extra bit of power to the plant's roots and it quivered, happy to have pleased him.

Or it could just be that she fit so damned well in their little slice of life, like she was always supposed to be here, and we are asshats trying to push her away for our own selfish protection.

Yeah, it was that. What kind of coward did that make him, all of them? With that sudden clarity, he made a decision. He didn't want her to go. Not now, not in two months. Never.

Shar spun on his heel. He needed to talk to his brothers, and then he needed to see his goddess, reassure her, make it clear that she was welcome, in whatever capacity she cared to take on. Whether that was lazing all day while he brought her berries to eat and Mell played music for her and Dub... well Dub would not be very good at letting her laze, but he would certainly make her beautiful things to wear. She could don armor and find a noble steed and gallivant all around the county seeking justice, stepping on toes and pissing off the Morrigan. She could drink tea and have visions and huddle next to a fire, and they would always make sure she was warm.

He could get her the puppy.

Shar pushed through the gate, never seeing the shadow that crept behind him. But he felt the knife as it plunged into his shoulder.

He fell to the pavement, the basket of berries slipping from his grasp.

One strawberry, of a perfect red ripeness, rolled to a rest in front of him as his vision faded.

Chapter Eighteen

Bastie,

The most horrible thing happened tonight. My giant...

I do not have the words. But I am growing attached to these not-men, and am beginning to dread the time when my two months are up.

Could it have been these men the visions were trying to show me, and not the place?

- Bat

BAT

*B*at jumped up. It was back, that feeling. It was here.

Where?

Her gaze darted around the room, trying to get a handle on the direction of the feeling.

She froze. *Shar. Where was Shar?* Shit, he'd left, gone out the back. She had pretended to ignore him, still mad at the treatment he and his brothers were giving her, but she'd been very aware of his movements.

She was beginning to think of them as *hers*.

Which was silly. A few offerings did not a worshipper make.

Even Dano, if she was truthful with herself, had only given her some boots. He probably had simply been being nice to a wet and cold traveler, and it had nothing to do with her being a goddess.

She grabbed Finn's arm and the vision of him in the alley returned to her.

Fudge. That was *now*.

"We need to get outside. Now. It's here."

Mell and Dub, who had risen when she did, rushed to the back. "Shar!" Dub called out.

Bat yanked again on Finn. "He's going to need you."

Finn moved reluctantly, and Bat growled. "No time for your games, warrior. Move." She pulled at his arm and pushed with her power, all the reserves she had, and he moved. Ailis came close behind them, Bat suspected to push the guardi as needed.

"Water."

At Bat's word, Ailis veered off to the sink.

Bat didn't wait. Her new friend would take care of that detail. She needed to get to Shar.

Bursting through the back door, she practically flew down the stoop, never letting go of Finn. A dark mound lay in the alley, still. Two figures stood over it, shrouded in shadow. Then one of them moved, and Bat recognized the angry movements of Dub.

"Get over here Cumhaill. Now." Those growled tones were familiar as well.

If Dub wanted them, that meant Shar was still alive. Bat took in a deep breath as she dragged the guardi over to her giant. And, yes, he was hers. To Ammat's jaws with anyone who said otherwise. For the next two months, these brothers were *hers*.

She yanked Finn to Shar's side. "Heal him."

"I need the water." Finn's voice was stiff, and his head twisted back and forth, searching.

"It's not here anymore. They must have fled as soon as they attacked Shar." Bat's fingers dug into the man's arm.

Flash. A masculine hand, holding the soul blade. A woman with red-gold hair kneeling, her tearful gaze shining up, green eyes deep as pools and just as mesmerizing. She held out a hand. "Please." The dagger wavered.

Bat threw off the vision. She'd look at it later. She'd look at all of them later, and demand the answers. There was a reason she kept seeing this woman.

Ailis arrived with the water. Bat snatched the glass from her and turned to Finn. "Water."

"He needs to drink it from my hands."

"Turn him over."

As Dub and Mell struggled with their brother's body, Bat knelt, pulling Finn down with her. Something firm squished under her knee. She saw the small basket and the strawberries that lay scattered in the alley.

175

Oh, my giant.

She sent a sharp look at Finn. "Hands."

He held out his hands, cupped, and she poured the water into them. Dub propped Shar up on his thighs, so the giant's head was tilted slightly forward. Mell held his mouth open.

"Come on, Shar, my giant, drink. Please drink. Drink for me now." Bat barely heard her own words, she was so focused on the slight trickle of water that ran from Finn's hands and to Searbhan's lips. Most of it continued down and ran off into his beard, but some made it into his mouth.

At first, nothing happened, and Bat scrambled for Shar's hand, hoping to sense something of his soul, or maybe give him some of her power. Except she had used it all getting Finn out here, and she had nothing more to give.

Her chest tightened, and a shaky breath escaped her.

Then she felt it. A soft pulse of life. It was leaking from the big man through a hole in the very fabric of his soul. His spirit was damaged, but intact.

"More." She handed the glass of water to Ailis who carefully poured more into Finn's hands. Again, a slow trickle worked its way into his mouth.

This time he swallowed.

But the wound was still there. This was nothing so simple as a physical stabbing. That was probably already healed. Bat dug deep, searching for what she could give. Her power was gone, but what if she gave something of herself, of her very essence? Didn't she do that with each supplicant she had ever had? They gave of themselves, and she gave back.

That was how it worked, or how it should. Even the storm gods—and the gods of evil and darkness and chaos —gave of themselves, not just their power.

But it took a sacrifice. More than an offering, a sacrifice required the giving up of something beloved, something that was essentially of the other person, or it required the death of something important. She *had* to have the exchange; she could not simply give, not this.

She shifted, and the juice of the berry under her knee seeped through her tights.

The strawberries. Harvested with care and love. He'd plucked them, had been on his way back to the pub. Normally these would merely be an offering, but... It wouldn't allow her to give much of herself, but maybe it would be enough. She could make the strawberries work, for this. For this, she *would*.

"Hand me a strawberry." She eyed the level of water in Finn's hands and in the glass. "And get more water. He's not gone, but he's not safe, not yet." When no one moved, her voice barked out. "Now."

Ailis bolted up the steps of the stoop and through the back door. Mell scooped up a berry, pausing to wipe it on his pants, and handed it to her.

The fruit was dirty, the sacrifice marred, but still pure of intention.

It would do.

Bat bit into it and felt a trickle of power leak into her. But it was the more shallow power of belief, of an offering, and was not what she sought. She swallowed.

There it is. The sacrifice of a supplicant, come seeking her favor. It was different and more powerful. It was an exchange.

What she thought of as her essence, different from the souls of mortals—and immortals—yet somehow the same, opened and a piece broke off. She guided it to the tear in Shar's spirit, laying it over the wound like a balm.

"Water," she whispered.

Ailis, back from the kitchen, poured more into Finn's hands and the red-haired man once again trickled the life-giving liquid into lips that were starting to gain color. The mouth opened further, and Shar's tongue darted out, licking droplets that sat on his lips. Finn tilted his hands, and the trickle became a stream. Shar's throat worked, taking in every bit of water.

The wound closed. Bat examined it with her mind's eye. A scar remained, a rough patch in his soul. Shar would never forget what had happened, it would haunt him, but he would live.

"Thank you." Bat whispered the words, though she didn't know to whom.

And something answered, spoke to her, just as it had on her first night here. A warm breeze caressed her face and a kind voice sounded through her.

You are very welcome, child.

For a moment she was cradled in Mother Sky's arms, and her essence was opened to the stars above. Bat held Shar to her and soared.

She came back to herself slowly, comforted by the knowledge that no matter where she was, the heavens were above her, holding back the chaos. Her hand crept to

Shar's chest and the steady thump of his heart, and the sense of him comforted her as well.

One last thing to do.

Through Shar, she reached for his garden.

She had never been an agricultural deity. Fertility in that regard was reserved mostly for the gods in her land, but the small aspect she did hold allowed her to offer Shar's garden some peace as she assured his *babies* that he would be okay. One bush, the one with the pink roses, bore the touch of another, but it was benign, and she let it be.

"We should get him inside now." Bat sat back on her heels.

Dub shifted, getting his arms hooked under his brother's while Mell took the feet. It was a little awkward, but maybe it was the only way the giant not-man could be moved?

A hand appeared before her, broad and covered in light golden hair, the same hand clutching the soul blade in her latest vision. She tilted her head back and met Finn's eyes.

He cleared his throat. "Thank you. For ensuring I made it to him in time. And, I am sorry you felt you had to. I... did not mean to hesitate. But I—I want you to know that I would not have refused to heal him, whatever you may have heard of me. Searbhan was, at one point, one of my best men and is still an honorable warrior."

Bat took the offered hand and allowed Finn to pull her to her feet.

"Shall I offer you something in return for your honesty?" She tilted her head and studied him, a man damaged by something she only yet had an inkling of. As soon as Shar was recovered, she would be sure to find out the whole of it. From all of them.

Finn looked away and his lips thinned. After a moment he nodded and met her eyes once more. "Please."

Oh my, please-s and thank you-s and sorry-s. Not something a fae offered lightly, or so she assumed. "You will have a choice to make soon, warrior of the light. Remember there are many kinds of beauty in this world, just as there are many forms of darkness, and of evil."

She turned away, Ailis by her side, and made her way to the pub. She left Ailis in the kitchen and climbed the stairs, searching each room until she found the brothers.

Shar lay like a still mountain, the movement of his chest the only physical sign he lived. She stepped up beside Dub and reached out, skimming a light hand over Shar's shoulder. He still wore his sweater and jeans, though his shoes were off.

"Do you think he would mind if I slept beside him? I would... like to be close to ensure there are no complications."

"What happened? We saw Finn give him the water, but it wasn't helping. I could... feel it." Mell's voice was tense.

Bat kept the tremble from her own voice by sheer will. "The blade tore his soul open. It was not just the flesh that needed to be healed, but the spirit as well." Her finger traced a circle over what she could reach of Shar's chest. "He will bear a scar."

Dub pulled in a sharp breath beside her. His hand nudged at her own, the one not touching his brother, and she turned her palm to him, lacing her fingers through his.

"Will he—" Mell broke off and swallowed. She could sense the emotion in him, beating at a wall he'd put up too hastily and that threatened to topple at any moment.

"He will be fine. He needs to rest. And so do you both," she said.

Dub squeezed her hand and let go. "I think he would very much enjoy you sleeping beside him." He walked to the door, pulling Mell after him. Just before exiting he turned back and bowed low to her. "We will resume the hunt on the morrow, goddess."

His words rang with power, the formality of them taking on the sound of ritual.

Bat nodded, and he closed the door. She would count on them to do something with Finn and Ailis. Right now, she needed to be beside her giant. Tomorrow would be soon enough.

She found a fluffy comforter on a shelf in the closet and lay down next to him, spreading the blanket over them both. She watched him as he slept, his beard stark against his too pale skin, his lapis eye closed. But his chest continued to rise and fall.

He would be okay.

Chapter Nineteen

Bastie!

He asked me to stay! The giant pirate one!

But…

I do wish you were here. You would know what I should do.

- Bat

BAT

*B*at didn't sleep. She spent the night watching and cuddling under the fluffy blanket. For that reason, she knew the exact moment Shar awoke.

His good eye blinked open and he sucked in a deep breath. Then he stiffened, blinked again, and turned his head to face her. "Good morning?"

"Hi." She propped her head up on one hand.

He blinked again. "I'm alive?"

Bat smiled. "Yup." She liked the informality of the sound and decided she would adopt more casual language as a rule. Though, right this moment, anything would sound good.

Shar was awake.

"I was stabbed."

Though he did seem to be having some trouble with the sequence of events. *Had his memory been affected?*

Bat reached out and felt his forehead. He flinched slightly, and she bit her lip. He didn't feel hot, or feverish, though he *was* warm.

"Yer hands are cold."

She pulled away a few centimeters and hesitated. Then she placed her palm against his chest. "I am always cold here."

One of his hands came up and enveloped hers, warming her, sending heat up her arm and through her whole body.

What?

Shar smiled at her, wide and calm, though there was a new shadow there. "Did I not mention I could warm ya very well, little goddess?"

She laughed, delighted with his teasing. Then she sobered. "I am so glad we made it to you in time. I didn't feel it right away. They must have moved so quickly..."

He twisted onto his side and wrapped an arm around her, pulling her into him, wrapping her in his warmth. "Shhh, shhh. You got there, did ya not? And ya brought Finn. I feel fine. Good as new even. Shhh."

She snuggled into him, allowing him to comfort her. A few more moments before the hunt resumed wouldn't be the end of all things, after all. They lay together, not moving, not speaking. She breathed him in, noticing he smelled of green and growing things underneath the day-old sweat and lingering aroma of pipe smoke and Guinness.

"Can I ask you something?" His chest vibrated against her ear as he spoke, tickling her.

She pulled back. His eye was trained on something past her, and slightly glazed, not really seeing the room.

"Of course."

"What did your visions show you? The ones that led you here." He focused on her and ran a large hand down her hair, resting his warm palm at the indent of her waist.

She snuggled back into him, her cheek against his chest, slightly irritated that he was clothed. What would his bare skin feel like? Thoughts she'd not allowed herself all night crowded in on her.

She was drawn to all three brothers. The kiss with Dub, Mell's ability to embrace both the pain and joy, Shar's calm and steadiness a balance against his more volatile brothers. But to act would upset the balance of *their* lives and bring more pain than joy.

But a goddess could dream...

Unbidden, her hand moved, pulling up his sweater just enough she could lay her fingers along the flesh of his back. She kept them light, barely there, skimming over the top of his pants.

He drew in a breath but otherwise didn't move.

Satisfied for the moment with this sign of welcome, Bat decided to answer his question. "They were not very clear. Mostly glimpses of a land that was green, one moment clouded and the next bathed in light. Some showed rainbows, some fields broken by stone walls, and others were of cliffs that fell into a crashing sea." She rubbed the tips of her fingers over his skin and he let out a heavy breath, pressing her into him. "Then I saw a sign. It wasn't much, a street sign. Bastet helped me research, and it led us here, to Sligo."

Giving in to impulse, she placed a soft kiss against his chest, too light for him to feel through his sweater. "I almost did not come here, despite it all. But then I had one more vision after Bastet found your advertisement for a room. In a way, it was even more unclear than the others, but in another, it was more illuminating. And compelling. There were only three things. A pint glass. The feeling that true home gives: hope, and peace, and comfort, and the knowledge that you can finally rest. And a hand held out in supplication and need."

She pushed away from him and tilted her head back, seeking his gaze, needing to watch his face as she said this last. "I think I may have found that here. Home. It's not a thing I have felt in millennia. But you and your brothers..." She lifted her hand from his side and cradled his cheek in her palm, the rough silk of his beard inviting her fingers to caress. "You, and this place, I have felt more at home with than any in my memory." Her thumb smoothed over his lips. "And, I thank you for it."

His good eye glowed, the lapis tones bright. His face was tight, and she couldn't read it, or him. Then he smiled, the slow, gentle one that made her want to snug into his arms and never leave. He curled forward and placed his lips on her forehead. Her eyes closed, and she sank into the moment, the perfect moment.

When he pulled back, she almost insisted he come back to her. But his face was back to serious, and she braced herself.

"Stay." It was one word, but it cut through her.

"I'm here for two more months, according to the terms of the rental." Was that a hitch in her voice? She pulled her hand into her own chest.

"Stay. You can work in the pub. I'll show you how to pull a pint. Mell would welcome a regular music partner. It would give Dub a break, and a chance to work on his projects. It would give me more of a chance to work with my garden and the wood. I've missed it. And..." The corner of his mouth quirked up. "And you fit with us, Bat, she of the two faces. You've stirred us up and brought life back to my brothers. Stay, little goddess."

She bit her lip and his gaze followed the movement. "What about the Morrigan? And the harp? And the soul blade and the offerings? All the reasons you gave, your brothers gave, for me to go, to not get involved?"

Shar groaned and his eye slid closed. He pulled her back to him, closing the small bit of distance she had put between their bodies. "We are wankers."

She smiled at the use of one of her favorite words but couldn't let this go. "All those reasons are still there, whether you are a wanker or not. I upset the balance. And that... has never been my purpose. I am meant to restore it. My presence in your land has only brought strife."

"No, the strife was there already. What is that saying, 'skinning cats to make a coat'?"

Her head reared away from him, horror pulling her mouth open and anger churning in her belly. "You skin cats here?"

"What? No. It's just a saying. I don't even know what it means. I would never actually... Crap."

Bat settled back against him. "Maybe the one with the eggs and the omelet?"

"Break a few eggs to make an omelet?"

"Yes, this one. We will use this one instead of the one of cats." She huffed. "The very idea."

He chuckled, and they fell back into silence.

Finally, she answered him. "I will think on it, on staying past the two months." There was one very important thing he had not brought up, something they would need to discuss before she made a final decision. Now was not the time for it, though, there were too many other things to settle.

"That's all I ask." A pause. "What happened after I was healed?"

"I do not know. I have been here all night."

The arm around her tightened, pressing the softness of her body against his. She felt the hard length of him, and almost pressed back, but...

"Since you are feeling so much better, it is time to get up. We have a soul stealing blade to track down. That is, if you are done being a wanker."

He gave her a final squeeze and let her go, rolling away from her. "For now, at least. No promises for the future."

The words bounced in her mind. *No promises for the future.*

No, there were never any real promises, were there?

Chapter Twenty

Bastet,

I met the most infuriating man last night. He is another one of these immortals, except not the same kind. Which is strange, because they all look like the same kind, except for his hair, which is more the color of Seth's.

I'm getting more answers this morning, but it looks like we are hunting not just something that can render the second death instantly (did we really not know of these things, it's horrific!) but someone who is twined through the pasts of my not-men.

Wish me luck!

- Bat, the determined goddess

BAT

*B*y the time she and Shar had showered and made their way to the lower floor, only Ailis was there, sitting at the bar. She jumped to her feet as they entered.

"Ye're awake!" She rushed up to them and, after a brief hesitation, wrapped her arms around Shar's middle and squeezed. Then she turned to Bat and did the same thing. "I was worried."

Bat hugged her back. Other than the few she'd received from the brothers, and the occasional ones from Bastet in her more gregarious moods, Bat didn't receive hugs. She decided she enjoyed them.

"Finn found a trace from last night. They're out tracking it down, asked me to keep an eye out for ya and make sure you were after eating before we head out. To join them," Ailis said. She grabbed Bat's hand and tugged her into the kitchen, where bread and jam were laid out. "Sit. Start. I'll whip up some sausages and eggs."

Bat tugged her hand free. "We should be out there with them."

Ailis busied herself pulling out a carton of eggs and package of sausage from the fridge. "No. What you should do is continue to recover your strength. Both of ya."

Shar placed a warm hand on her shoulder. "She's right. We rested last night and we lingered this morning. Half an hour to eat is smart."

Bat knew he was correct, but she'd been eager to get back to it, and not just to find Dano's killer. No, the sooner this was resolved, the sooner she could make some decisions about her own future. She nodded and Shar squeezed her shoulder.

"Good," he said. "I'm going to go pick some berries. You get the tea started." He gestures to the small tin of bags that sat on the counter.

Her chest tightened. "Maybe I can go for the berries? You make the tea? You are very good with the tea."

Shar narrowed his good eye at her, and she braced herself for a fight. Then his shoulders eased down and his lips quirked. "Just this once. If they give you any trouble, tell me."

Bat's mind filled with images of brambles and roots wrapping around her limbs to drag her into the soil. "Um. Maybe I will make the tea. You go reassure your babies that you're fine. I'm paying attention now. I'll know if anything sneaks up on us."

"They went ahead and warded the alley as well as the garden," Ailis put in.

"Oh, that's all right then," Bat said to Shar. "You go out to the garden."

He raised a brow and smirked, looking very much like a pirate. "You were worried about me."

She stared at him. "Of course, I was worried about you. Your spirit has a *scar*."

He shrugged and was out the door.

Ailis nudged her shoulder and held out a plate. "Take this. Sit. Start. I'll have some hot food for ya in a few. And those brothers... well, they are pretty resilient, ya know."

Bat took the plate but didn't move. "I don't know.

There is a lot that went unsaid last night. That needs to change today."

Ailis averted her gaze and tucked a strand of her green hair behind her ear. "Ye're right. But some tales are not mine to tell, and as much as I like a good gab, that story is one." She looked at Bat then, the wicked light back in her eyes. "But I'll help hold them down and hand you the pliers if they refuse to talk."

"I'm sure torture will not be necessary." Bat wasn't sure of any such thing. "But I do appreciate the offer." She set the plate on the island and busied herself with making tea. She was very good at being patient, even when she didn't want to be.

It wasn't long before her belly was full and dishes were piled in the sink to be washed later.

"So," she said. "Where are they now?"

As if in answer to her question, Shar's phone let out a low ping. He pulled it from his back pocket. "They've lost the trace out near Carney. Finn's asked us to meet them at the headquarters."

Ailis gave a sharp nod. "We can take my car. I'll be back in a few minutes. It's parked behind me shop."

Shar held up a hand. "We'll go with you. If they lost the trail, there is no telling where she—it—is."

Bat noted the correction, but let it go, for now. She'd rather confront them all at once over the topic than wrestle with stubborn men four different times. Exchanging a look with Ailis, they nodded to each other and headed out.

Unlike yesterday, when the sun seemed determined to shine down, today the clouds hovered, and a light mist rested in the air, coating her in damp. The boots—along with a thick pair of socks she'd found in her drawers this morning—certainly helped, but when this was over, she would definitely need to find some gloves. And a scarf. And maybe a thicker coat. Or she would simply haul a fire around with her everywhere she went and—

Shar grabbed her hand and warmth flowed up her fingers. "You were shivering," he said, and left it at that.

Today the streets were quiet. Pedestrians and passersby hurried about on errands, and a few stopped to tilt their caps or nod a greeting at Ailis. The occasional flapping steamer met Bat's gaze, but for the most part, the city had recovered from the celebrations. Storefronts sported neat displays. Bookstores, confectionaries, boutiques, even a pharmacy. It was very different from her home, but she liked it.

Ailis led them down a narrow alley and stopped beside a small green car. It looked like a bubble more than a car, really, but there were four wheels, seats and a steering wheel, so Bat assumed it would work.

"I can't fit in that," Shar said, crossing his arms. "I can port us there."

"Eh, no," Ailis countered, crossing her arms as well. "I don't trust that druid magic. Imagine making little symbols and relying on those to take ya places instead of using what you were born with." She gave a little shudder.

Bat examined the vehicle again. "I could sit in the back, behind Ailis," she offered. That would probably work. Shar could push the front seat all the way back and... it wouldn't be comfortable, that was sure. Maybe he could do this porting thing, and she and Ailis would meet him there?

He groaned. "Fine. But no way am I letting myself be seen like this. I'm masking."

Ailis shrugged and climbed into the car. "Just you. I don't want anyone running into me because they couldn't be bothered to see me."

Bat climbed in after her and then watched in fascination as Shar pushed the passenger seat back and folded his frame into the too tight space. His knees were practically up around his shoulders, and he had to duck his head down to avoid hitting the ceiling.

She giggled. His grimace made him look so much like Dub, and then she imagined the older brother in a similar situation, and it just... slipped out.

He glared. "It is glad I am that I can amuse you so."

He didn't sound glad. She sobered, or tried to, but when she opened her mouth to apologize another laugh came instead. His frown intensified, and he turned away from her, glaring first at Ailis then out the front windshield. Then he did something with his fingers, traced them over the dash and... disappeared.

Bat narrowed her eyes and concentrated. He was still there, but... fuzzy. The longer she looked, the clearer he became, but he never quite focused.

Ailis started the car. "Weird, isn't it?"

It was magic, not the same power Shar laid claim to through his nature, but borrowed power. Bat realized that the little flicks of his fingers must have been a sort of ritual. Fascinating. Who did he call upon? Heka? But, no, that was an Egyptian name. What did the Irish call the father of magic, who pervaded all things? Surely this was the same being in all the lands, though it would go by different names?

"You are a sorcerer?" she asked.

Shar shifted, cramming his arm between his seat and knee, and scratched his head. "Not really. We've picked up a few useful things from the Druids over the years."

Bat tilted her head. These she had read of in the Idiot's Guide. They were much like the priests and healers of her own land. She nodded in understanding. These immortals, some of them at least, utilized more than one type of power. Was this also how the soul blade worked?

She settled back against the seat and watched the shops and buildings flash by. She would hold her questions for just a little longer.

The guardi's headquarters were not what she had been expecting. She surveyed the corrugated metal walls. They were in fairly good shape, but there were spots of rust on a few panels, and the windows that lined the upper edges were dirty. A small loading dock sat behind a chain fence, and a metal safety door was the only entrance.

Bat stepped out of the car, soon followed by Shar, who more shoved himself from the tight confines. Then he just... walked through the gate. Bat looked closer. It held the same fuzziness that disguised Shar. So, the reverse? A fence that wasn't there but was?

Intriguing. She was coming to recognize the signs of this tracing magic.

She followed him and felt a pressure and a slight pop, very similar to what she'd experienced the first time she'd stepped over the threshold of the pub. There was no rush afterward, but the initial resistance was the same.

What greeted her was not the same as the concrete loading area she'd seen from the street. A neat lawn, with stone paths winding through it and bushes at strategic areas, gave the warehouse a softer look. The bushes rustled, and a small figure, no more than the length of her palm, darted up and over to her. Rapid wing beats lent an impression of an aura around the tiny body, blue and green and purple swirled together. It hovered in front of her face, the loose clothing disguising its sex, but she got the impression of a definite masculinity from the way the creature held its shoulders.

"Hello," she said. Why did Egypt not have anything as delightful as this?

It darted around her, surveying her from many angles then returned to her face. "Hello," it finally said, the voice small and high, but still very understandable. "Will you come play for us some time? I've a cousin who heard ya the other night, and she said it was lovely."

Bat tilted her head. "I would like to say yes, but I am not sure if I will be welcome in this place after we are done with our investigation."

The figure folded its arms. "Well, I'm in charge of this particular territory. You just come here, and we'll have a sing and a listen, and none need go anywhere near the building for the bigs."

Bat grinned. "Agr—"

"*A stor*. Goddess." Shar stepped in front of her. "Do not—"

The figure flew at Shar, and it no longer appeared so benign. "I know you, giant. Unworthy, you are."

Shar flinched but otherwise made no move to relent.

"We just want a listen, protector of the Rowan. We are pledged to guard this place and do not leave easily. A gesture of peace, let's call it, from the strange goddess. You may even accompany her."

Bat laid her hand on Shar's back and pressed.

He relaxed. "It will need to wait—"

"Until the *lann de anam* is found, I know." The little figure waved a hand and zipped back to his bush.

"Damn pixies," Shar mumbled.

Bat stared after the figure. "That was a pixie? I thought Ciara was a pixie."

Ailis grabbed her hand and dragged her toward the door. "There's littles and bigs. Most stick to one size or the other, though all can change. Enough of that, now."

The door opened from the inside, revealing Finn framed in the doorway. The guardi Captain looked different. Resigned defeat pulled his shoulders down, and bruised circles sat under his eyes, but the set of his mouth told her he held a determination stronger than either the defeat or exhaustion. His gaze settled on Shar. Something passed between the two men, and Finn nodded. "It is glad I am to see you so well."

Shar inclined his own head in acknowledgment. "I hear I have you to owe for healing the wound in my shoulder."

Finn shrugged. "Nothing is owed for that. As the Morrigan told me, it is my mess to clean up."

Bat stepped forward. "I want answers now. I let it go before, but after what happened to Shar last night, I will have them." She didn't push her power out, though. She didn't have enough to spare, and really, it was only decent for them to concede the point.

Finn focused on her and she pulled in a breath. The purple around his eyes pulled forward the green rings around the edges of the irises so that they practically glowed. His expression went blank. He was not going to give her anything, it seemed. Then he inclined his head, verging on a bow, and motioned for them to enter. "Yes, it is time you had some answers, goddess."

Bat wasn't sure how to take his words, so she simply nodded and stepped forward. He led them through plain halls, past a pair of painted doors, and up a steep flight of stairs. Dub, Mell and another man waited at the top.

A thrill of mixed relief and excitement swept through her at the sight of the two brothers, and she sprinted the last few steps to throw her arms around Dub.

"Hey, what about me?" Mell inserted an arm between their bodies and plucked her away from his brother.

She enfolded him in her arms as well. Yes, hugs were good things. She would make sure she gave and received many more of these before... well, before.

"Well now, that's a sight." The third man hovered right beside them. "Never thought I'd see the day a Fomoiri hugged a goddess, especially an Egyptian one. More likely to try gutting them, they are."

Bat pulled her head from Mell's chest. What a rude thing to say. "And who are you to be making such proclamations?"

Finn held out his arms and ushered them all away from the top of the steps and down the hall. "This is Oisin. He's usually too charming for his own good, but we've had an influx of goddesses lately and it's thrown him."

Ailis nodded wisely. "He's having ruptions."

Oisin tilted his chin up. "I do not have 'ruptions' as you so eloquently put it. It was a simple observation."

It sure did not sound *very simple*. In fact, it sounded like yet another thing she didn't know of this land and which may impact her decision to stay.

The banter had taken them down yet another plain hallway until they stopped before a single door carved with letters and shapes Bat didn't know.

The red-haired Oisin waved his hand in a complicated pattern and then pushed the door open for her. "Welcome to *my* domain, goddess."

Wood shelves, polished to a dark sheen, lined the walls. In the center of the room, flanked by yet more shelves, stood a large table, tomes and books scattered across the surface. A few smaller desks were off to the right, modern computers and printers and office-y type things arranged neatly over them. To the right of the room was a line of cases, the glass wavering in her vision as though spelled. And inside the cases were yet more books.

Maybe there was a bit of the cat in her because suddenly all she wanted to do was examine whatever those cases contained. She even took a step in their direction before Mell, who still had an arm around her, pulled her back.

"Later, *realta*. I'm sure if you ask nicely, Oisin will let you play with his treasures." His voice was teasing, the tone a bit cruel, and his gaze was trained not on her but the red-haired man.

More history she didn't know. She sighed. And another reminder that she had a story to pry from the stubborn hands of these not-men.

She slid from under Mell's arm and took a seat near the head of the table. She'd leave the one on the end for Oisin out of courtesy for his position over this particular territory. "Now. We will get to the bottom of this situation."

Dub took the seat to her right, Mell and Shar taking the ones directly across from her, their movements reluctant. Finn sat beside Dub, Ailis across from him, and Oisin took the seat she'd left open for him.

No one spoke.

"Why don't we start with Benbulben?" she asked. An easy enough opening. She would give them one more chance before she forced the issue.

It was not a power she enjoyed using. She never had. But when, at the birth of her creation, she decided she would be an upholder of Ma'at, she gained not only the epithet of "the one who is saved" but a power other than her visions. She gave up much of herself each time it was employed, and therefore had let it lay dormant in herself even before the uniting of the kingdoms.

Strange how sometimes we come back to our selves. Her long existence had given her many roles, and here in this strange land, she found once more one of the first she had ever taken on.

"I can force the truth of this from you." She held up a

hand to forestall any protests. "I would prefer not to, for many reasons, not the least of which is I have always seen this as a... violation. Something done to criminals, and to... clear the air, I think is the term." She drew herself up in her seat. "I seek only one thing at the moment, and that is a soul blade and the one who wields it. Each of you hold pieces of the answer, and yet you keep them to yourselves. That is not justice."

Dub held his hand out to her, palm up.

She tilted her head in question.

"See what you can see, please. This is... has *never* been an easy thing for me to speak of."

She rubbed the tips of her fingers over the soft skin of Dub's wrist and sighed. "You will allow me to see what I may get from you?"

He didn't answer, but he did shift and thread his fingers with hers.

She took it as a final approval and reached out with her mind's eye.

Flash. A dark night. Dub, in leather armor and a red cloak, held a sword. A man, golden of hair and wild-eyed, stood clasping a child, a girl with freckles and red hair. To her throat, this man held a knife that glowed with a dark light, its hilt a serpent's head. Dub lunged, but he was too late, for the dagger plunged into the child's neck and ripped through her throat. The flesh paled, the freckles standing out in stark contrast, and the dagger glowed with a pale rose hue for a moment. The golden-haired man laughed, even as Dub slammed into him. Dub knocked his hand away from the dagger where it still stuck in the girl's neck and grabbed it himself. His expression dark, he plunged it into the madman's abdomen, then again in his chest, angling up to hit the heart. The man paled, and the blade glowed with a sickly red.

The value of a soul?

Flash. Benbulben. Sunlight streaming through the clouds, bathing the mountain in gold.

Bat strained for more, but that was all that was revealed to her.

She looked down at where her hand was joined to Dub's. Tanned and scarred, calluses on his palms and fingers from where he had gripped a weapon countless times. Bat lifted that hand to her mouth and placed a soft kiss on the knuckles.

He didn't ask what she saw, and she did not offer. He had, in his way, shown her what she needed to know. The blade that killed this man, Diarmuid, was the same that killed Dano and had last been seen beside a weeping woman.

One thing was clear, though. "This *does* come back to Benbulben. Every vision, everything I see, circles around to this place of your legends." She glanced at Dub, and he must have suspected what she saw and seen the question in her gaze, for he nodded. She tightened her fingers on his and looked at the others. "The soul blade used on Dano was the same as the one used on the golden-haired madman."

"Fuck." Mell ran a hand through his shaggy hair and sat back in his seat. He glared at Finn. "If you don't tell it, I will."

"Hold." Oisin raised his hand. "Let me confirm. It is why you wanted to meet here, after all. Many of the blades have a similar design."

Bat stiffened as this not-man she had just met rose from his chair and headed for one of the cases. She was done doubting herself, but why did these immortals continue to... He reached in and drew out a tome. Bound in worn and scraped leather, it was as thick as the width of her hand, the pages ragged. He carried it with gentle care and placed it before her with a soft whump. Then, again oh so carefully, he drew it open, flipping to a page of sketches. "Please, for our own formalities and records, identify the blade you saw." His voice was matter of fact. "We have certain procedures we must follow in this modern time."

"Oh." That made sense then. It only took her a few seconds to spot it. "This one." Even without the color of the stone, the tilt of the serpent's head was distinct. And Oisin was right, many of the blades had a similar look, and at least three others had a serpent.

"Thank you."

They waited as he returned the tome to its resting place.

"It is the same one," he said as he sat. "Finn, Mell is right. If you do not, we will need to."

Finn's fists clenched, the knuckles white. Bat could not see his expression, Dub blocked much of the view of the other man, but those hands told a story in themselves. "Grainne. The woman you are seeing. Her name was Grainne."

"Was?" Bat was careful to keep her voice even, not insensitive to those hands and their tale.

"Is. Was. I do not know."

She nodded, though he couldn't see her. "Is the deer also involved in this?"

Oisin grabbed her hand. "You've seen a deer?" His brown gaze drilled into her and his fingers would have left bruises if she had not been a goddess.

Flash. A doe, her eyes wide as she warily watched a little red-haired child approach, his clothes a rough and homespun linen.

Flash. A woman, with hair to match the boy's, fleeing across the fields below the half mountain of Benbulben. But she was not a woman, she was the doe, and she had been enchanted.

Oisin's hand sprang open and he snatched it way.

Ailis snorted. "No one really told her about your mother, but you just did."

"Sadb." Warmth infused Finn's voice, and his clenched hands eased. "No, Sadb is not involved in this. And Oisin, you need to let her go. I have."

Oisin made no answer, and again the guardi captain fell silent.

Ugh. This was like... like... like getting Bastet to do something she didn't want to do. What usually worked with the cat?

Bribery.

"I will share my strawberries with you if you will just tell me what happened." That should be sufficient.

Finn snorted and leaned forward to peer at her, one brow raised.

Maybe not. He did not understand the significance of strawberries obviously.

But his lips had quirked up and his hands were still relaxed.

"Enough." Shar shoved out his chair and rose. "A right bastard, was Diarmuid. He was Finn's nephew. Ran off with his fiancée. Or she ran off with him, in truth. Her father had arranged the match with Finn. Finn was going to let them go, Diarmuid had paid the price demanded by the Brehon, but then there were rumors of a new god haunting the forests." He hesitated, and something like shame clouded his expression. "I had a run in with him, in the Dubros. I was keeping the trees then, after..." He shrugged his shoulders. "Anyway, I was set to guard the Rowan, but he bested me, and destroyed it. And Grainne helped him. She..."

Bat could guess this one from his tone. "She seduced you." She also found it of note that no one refuted Shar's claim that Diarmuid was a bastard.

The big not-man lowered his gaze to the floor and gave the slightest nod.

"So, a pair of the wicked." Bat licked her lips. "She was beautiful?" She'd seen the visions of course, but the question slipped out. She didn't like the way her giant wouldn't meet her gaze.

"The loveliest creature born in twelve centuries, or since." Mell's voice was soft.

"You too?" Jealousy crept into her and nestled in, making itself at home.

Mell eyed her, then skimmed his gaze down her sweater covered body. "Well, maybe not the *loveliest*," he said, not answering. Then he sent her a wink, startling a laugh from her. "But, yes, she was lovely. I think most were half in love with her, though she was promised to Finn." His brown eyes glazed over, looking at something she hadn't seen yet. "In the end, she wanted Diarmuid. And he was a good kid, for all that. I don't know what happened, but he... twisted somewhere along the way."

Finn's hands clenched then flattened out. "Grainne happened to him."

The full picture was coming to her. "And no one knows what became of her?"

"I just wanted to forget," Finn said.

"We all did." Dub used his free hand to clasp the other man's shoulder. "And, no. No one knows what happened to her. Some say she decided to fade, to move on now that her love had gone. Some say they still see her on cold nights under Benbulben, others that she became a baobhan sith, and drinks of wicked men. But they are all rumors..."

"So, she could have had the blade, and given it to them." Bat kept her voice even. It had been right there. Right beside the woman. And if she would support a man who wielded a soul blade, she could also certainly be the type to use it herself. "And she could very well be here. I don't think my visions were simply trying to tell me one of the baboon sivs were using the soul blade, or they would have stopped after the first. No, I am seeing Benbulben for a reason. And her, I see her for a reason. She *is* here."

Finn rose, nodded to Oisin, and then strode from the room.

"He'll be back in a moment," Oisin offered. "More procedural things. He's got a portrait of her, so we can verify this is who you saw in your... visions."

There was so much wrong with that statement. Was Finn a danger to them, to the investigation? After all the woman had done, why would he keep a picture of her?

The air in the room thickened as they waited. Even Ailis held her words. Bat started piecing together what she'd seen in the visions and what she had been told, especially of the woman. There were things the men hadn't told her, she was sure, but she had enough to build that picture.

A woman who betrayed her intended. A woman who seduced and twisted and corrupted all for her own gain, and who quite likely enjoyed being adored—and if Bat was honest, who didn't want to be adored? But she'd also driven a young man to commit murder, then shown real grief over his slain body.

Finn appeared beside her, crowding in on her left. He set a portrait on the table before her. The paint was faded and peeling, but the woman depicted was clear.

"It's her."

Finn pulled the canvas away, his gaze lingering on it for a moment. Then he nodded, set the painting on the ground against one of the bookcases and returned to his seat. "So, we have confirmation. But you have not seen her wielding the blade?"

"No." *But I have seen you holding it.* She didn't say the last, an instinct holding her back. The flow of the threads of fate came together, and in the end, it had to be his decision. That was also very clear to her. "I do have one question. Why Dano? Why linger at the farmhouse and bother the pixie, why not simply take her as another victim? If her goal was to harness more power, then she is acting counter to that, unless there is something else in play." *And my earlier speculations that Dano was not the target were correct.*

"Vengeance." The word slipped from three mouths. Dub, Finn, and Shar stared at each other, and then Dub continued, emotion stripped from him. "She would want vengeance on me, for the death of her love."

Finn snorted. "More like thwarting her plans. That demon never knew love, not truly."

The words startled Bat. They were something she'd expect from Dub, not the man who could barely utter her name. Or maybe the words were simply coming out now.

"Yet *you* still love her," Mell said.

Finn leaned back and rubbed a hand over his face. "I love the idea of her. After Sadh, she was the bright promise. That the promise was a lie..." He shrugged. "I do not..."

"Well, you are going to need to let go of whatever attachment this is." Bat slammed her hand down on the table. "It is not easy, but you need to do it. You ask if I've seen her with the blade in her hands, but did you not track her from the alley after Shar was attacked? Was she not the last to be seen near it? Was she also not... *in cahoots* with her lover in the taking of lives? How was it she escaped justice the first time around?" Her heart pounded and her blood surged. She'd been patient, more than patient. She'd been gentle.

It was obviously not what this not-man needed. So, she would provide what he needed.

"Stop being a wanker," she said. "Stop being deliberately blind." She stood and placed her palms on the table, twisting to meet Finn's gaze. "Stop being a coward."

Finn's eyes glowed at her once more. It was a much better look for him.

"She destroyed everything she touched," Dub said, his tone even. He laid a hand on Finn's shoulder.

Finn didn't break his gaze from hers. Then he nodded. It was an acknowledgment. Not that he would "let go" as she had told him, but that he heard her, and he would try. "I will do what needs to be done," he said. "This time."

She nodded in turn.

Then she sat and focused on Oisin. Finn whispered something that may have been, "farking stars," but she ignored him.

"Tell me," she said to the not-man whose territory she was in. "Are there any more of these protocols we must adhere to? Or may we begin the search again?"

Oisin, eyes wide and darting around the room, inclined his head. "All protocols that must be observed for witness have been done. I will record your testimony."

"Oh goody," Ailis muttered.

"Yes, goody." Bat tapped the tabletop, thinking. "You lost the trace. Did you find anything of the babylon sit?"

"Baobhan sith," whispered Shar from beside her, but she waved him off.

She was on a roll, and not worried about

pronunciations. Excitement raced through her, sending her blood pumping. Her senses heightened, ready for the hunt. "I wonder if it was not the blade I have been sensing, but Grainne. I didn't feel anything the night Dano was killed, but I did at the farm when I was harmed by that rifle."

Mell leaned forward sharply. "Not the blade?"

"No." This made sense, much more sense. Objects were not the source of evil or chaos, only beings. "I think it was just her I sensed, the madness and the wrongness of her, outside of the farmhouse, and not the blade." Bat locked eyes with Finn once more. "She's a corruptor. Seeps in like poison."

Finn's eyes were wide, his face soft with a strange kind of hope. "No argument here. You think you can track her directly...?"

"If I am close enough. The feeling faded quickly. And to stop her, not to kiss her." Bat still felt that needed to be made clear.

Finn nodded, but that was his only reply. He'd once more gone silent. Bat would keep an eye on him. Once chaos got its claws in you, you had to dig it out, and that was hard work. It was much easier to keep it out in the first place.

Mell pushed back from the table and stood, Shar a beat behind him. "Well then, let's get this hunt started." Eagerness and a wild joy radiated from him. He grinned, and it held none of the comfort of his usual smiles. This was the warrior before her.

Beside him, Shar wore a matching expression, very

pirate-like. A shift of her head revealed Dub's frown held the same ferocious eagerness as his brothers' smiles.

One of her earlier visions came to her, of the brothers at the prow of a ship, hair windblown and bristling with weapons of all kinds.

Her heart pounded, and heat poured through her, both an answering need to hunt this piece of chaos down and eliminate it, and a lower heat.

Then Shar frowned. "I am not getting in that torture device Ailis claims is a car, and we don't have room in the truck for everyone."

Ailis stood as well and crossed her arms. "I can take my car on my own, thank you."

There was something wrong with that, something Bat should remember...

"No." Finn rose as well, so the only one still seated was Oisin. "No, I have a vehicle. None of us should be alone until this is resolved, even you, fairy. Grainne has no doubt seen you with us and will target you if given the opportunity."

He barely flinched at the use of his former fiancée's name. Progress.

But there was something new there as well. A different kind of veil. Bat glanced at Mell and raised a brow. He sent back a brief sense of caution. She'd been correct, Finn was not dealing well with this.

Ailis glanced between the three of them then nodded. "Fine. I'll ride with ya. But you better not try anything tricky with those finger wiggles. Damned Tuatha, meddling in things that should be left alone," she muttered the last. Then she headed out the door.

Mell and Shar followed. Bat was nearly to the door when she paused and spun around, catching Finn and Dub in mid-stride. There was something else that hadn't been touched upon in the discussion. And that was the young man she assumed both had once counted as a friend, from the way they spoke of him. "You should know that it could not have ended any other way with Diarmuid," she said. The words were for both Finn and Dub. A small gift from a goddess, unsolicited, so it fit the rules. "The death. It could not have ended any other way. What you knew of that man would have long been gone, eaten away." It was not much, but it was something. "He was already dead before the blade ever touched him, before the hunt ever commenced."

She stayed there, blocking the way until they nodded. She didn't know if they believed her words, and often what the heart accepted was not the same as what the mind accepted. She made a note to tell them as many times as necessary for all the parts of them to believe her words. For they were true.

She spun on her boots and headed after the others.

There was a hunt to conduct.

Chapter Twenty-One

Bastie,

I learned to do something tonight I can guarantee none of the other gods know how to do, even Bes. I now know how to pull a proper pint of Guinness!
Hah!

- Bat, the NEW goddess of beer

BAT

"Maybe we should call the Wild Hunt?"

"Those maniacs? *No.* Not happening. They'll just go on a rampage, with no discretion whatsoever. Remember what happened with…"

Bat left Finn and Mell to their discussion in the kitchen and moved to the pub proper. Shar was there behind the counter. Dub had accompanied Ailis back to her shop and the apartment above it so that she could fetch some essentials for the night.

When there had been no further sign of Grainne or the baobhan sith—*ha! Got it right*—they had come back to the pub to... regroup, Finn had called it. After searching the roads and back trails to and from Carney, and around, each agreed a different strategy was needed. There was nothing efficient about having six people going around together, following trails that ended in circles.

What was frustrating for Bat, was the fact she couldn't get a sense of Grainne at all. Her range was dismal. Which meant they were relying on Finn to track her. The brothers seemed to take his assurances at face value that he had lost the trail, or where it led them, but Bat wasn't so sure. Or, not so sure that his own mind wasn't playing tricks on him.

Ailis had once again started talking about taking another tack—getting a bunch of the fae together to bring offerings and give Bat a boost. Technically, that was within the bounds of what the Morrigan laid out, but it violated the... spirit of the agreement, and Bat was not yet ready to do that. She might be closing a door she wanted kept open.

But if something didn't happen soon to show them the way to this blade, she would certainly contemplate the strategy with true intention.

It also struck her as strange that the Morrigan was not more involved in the hunt for this blade. Surely this was just the type of thing a deity should become involved in?

"Little goddess, come here and let me show you a few things." Shar beckoned to her from behind the bar.

Could she be blamed if her mind went to those things of his she would like to be shown? "What wonderful things do you have for me, giant of the forest?" Maybe she had decided to tackle the question of the brothers and her attraction to them after Grainne was dealt with, but a little light teasing had never harmed.

He blushed. *Oh my*.

Then he grinned. "Not that. I'm going to show ya how to pull a pint proper." He grabbed up one of the glasses kept under the counter, the same ones she'd helped clean just last night.

She stepped up beside him. There had been a ritual to Dub's actions last night, very precise movements. Was it a form of magic in itself to produce the drink so many of the patrons had enjoyed?

"Now just watch this time. Hold the glass just so, at this angle." He tipped the curved glass to forty-five degrees. "Now, ya pull the tap forward. Not back, mind ya. That comes later." He grasped the handle to release the beer. "When it gets to... here, start straightening the glass." It was upright before he even finished speaking. "Now to let it settle. The settling's important." He set it down.

She stared at the glass as the cloudy liquid gradually cleared to a deep brown and a white foam formed at the top.

"Now." Shar picked the glass. "Ya top it off, just so." He pushed the tap away this time, instead of pulling it toward him.

"That is quite a ritual. But I can do that. I understand about precision in religious practices." She eyed the glass, then the tap, then how Shar stood, trying to memorize it all.

He laughed. "Oh, it's not religious, though some may argue. And it's not magic. But some things are best done with precision and care, do ya not think?" His hand slipped around her waist and drew her in.

"Ahem."

Shar glanced up and his grin grew. He didn't let her go, though.

Bat twisted. Dub and Ailis stood there, Ailis with a grin and a pillow clutched in her arms, Dub with a frown and two bags. Bat had teased once that she was beginning to understand his frowns. This one wasn't angry. It was more... speculative.

Ailis wagged her brows. "So, am I getting yer room all to myself tonight? I was afraid I'd have to share but doesn't look like I'm the one to be doing the sharing."

Bat pushed away from Shar. "No." This was the conversation she wasn't yet ready to have, about thoughts and urges she had barely acknowledged even to herself. She was in the midst of redefining herself. She would not take a miss-step with these men and risk becoming like the woman they hunted, concerned with only her own wants and desires. "No, Ailis, I am afraid you will need to share with me this night. I will try not to hog the covers." She grinned, in part at Ailis's overly disappointed expression but also at the image conjured, of a pig swathed in blankets, rolling on the floor.

Dub's eyes narrowed but he didn't speak, and moments later he and Ailis headed up the narrow stairs to the level above.

Shar nudged her. "I apologize, goddess. I would not want to make unwelcome advances." The flush was back on his cheeks, and his tone held disappointment and a little shame.

She laid a hand on his muscled forearm. "It is my place to apologize in this. I should not have teased. Not after that kiss with your brother." *And especially after my own protests against upsetting the balance of your lives.*

"Is it Dub ya want then?" He looked down at the pint he'd just pulled, staring as though the dark liquid would hold the answers of the stars above. Or the answers to her.

It was still not a time to discuss such things. "Ask me again after we have caught Grainne and recovered the blade." She looked up at him, and her chest tightened. Had she just made a mess of things? Done the exact thing she'd promised herself she would not?

He pulled in a breath, stretching the sweater so it outlined the muscled bulk of his chest, then released it in a rushed exhalation. He nodded. "I want you. I will not hide that. I want to pull you in, to sink into you and revel in the sheer beauty of your form and your very being. The gods of Egypt must be fools to have let you go, to have let you become so diminished." The gaze of his lapis eye captured her. "And I still want you here, to stay with us. We will care for you as they never did. But, you are also correct, now is not the time to speak of such things. We cannot be distracted in the coming days, and that is what my brothers and I will be if we go down this path. I will speak with them."

Bat looked down. "Thank you." Then she peeked up at

him. "Is it true 'thank you' is considered an insult? I read it in my guide, and I don't want to keep insulting everyone, but it slips out sometimes."

Shar's chest shook with suppressed laughter. "It is not an insult," he finally managed. "But it does imply a debt. If you keep thanking everyone, you'll be owing more favors than you can grant."

Her eyes went wide. "Oh." Her mind scrambled, trying to remember everyone she'd said "thank you" to since she'd arrived. Was it for all Irish or just the immortals? If it was for all Irish, she most likely owed that first bus driver the equivalent of a first-born.

"Eh, ya should be safe enough in general, but I wouldn't go making any promises to the sluagh. They've stuck to the old ways, and would demand blood, or worse, most likely." With a lift of his shoulders, he stretched his neck. "Now, back to what I wanted to teach you in the first place." He waved at the tap. "You try."

She picked up a pint glass. "Will you tell me of the different immortals? I will admit there are so many names thrown out, I am having trouble keeping track of them."

And in this way, her education of this land continued, as she practiced the pulling of a pint and learned the intricacies of Irish immortals.

It was almost as confusing as the hierarchy of the Egyptian deities. There were Fir Bolg and sluagh, who were almost the same thing, except Fir Bolg could also simply mean the ancient humans who had lived on the green isle before the coming of the Tuatha. The sluagh were said to be the restless and lost souls of those humans, and stuck to the dark, preferring the bogs and deep forests. They rode with the wild hunt and claimed the souls of others lost to ride with them forever. Even the Fomoiri and Tuatha didn't know their true nature, for they had been the true original inhabitants of the land. They had their own social structure and could be dealt with, but even the deities tended to leave them alone.

Then came the Tuatha and the Fomoiri and the fae. Trooping fairies and solitary fae and all manner of things wicked in the night as well as beautiful in the sun. Oh, and the Celts and the Druids. The peoples had become so mixed over the centuries that the labels themselves were more to distinguish family lines or allegiances more often than not. Many of the more wild and solitary fae, such as the pooka she had met, or leprechauns like Dano, were still identified by their powers.

"The Fomoiri, now, we're a little different. Most tend to stick to the seas, and traveled long until finally settling around the north and west of Ireland." Shar watched as she topped off her fifth pint. This one looked much closer to his original one. They were all lined up on the bar. Some cloudy all the way through, one with the sharp line of foam and beer though Shar said there was not enough of the foam for a balance of taste, and others with gradients from dark to light.

She set this one at the end of the line and admired the neat divide of dark and light and how the liquid rounded just slightly above the lip of the pint glass.

"Good," he said. "You'll get it yet."

Bat smiled up at him, and only then noticed Mell and Dub, hovering at the edge of the bar. She gestured to the pint glasses, her movements radiating challenge.

"I get that last one," Mell said, and moved to claim a stool at the bar.

Bat swept it up. "No. Shar gets this one because he's been teaching me while you argue over things with the guardi."

"Is that all I am?" Finn, followed by Ailis, stepped in from the hall.

She didn't answer. Instead, she brought them back to topic. "Have you fierce warriors decided where we will hunt next?" Yes, she was needling the guardi, but something about him, an inherent arrogance, got her back up.

Shar picked up the original pint he'd pulled and set it in front of Bat, so the only options left to the others were her cloudy first attempts. Dub sighed but picked up the one that was her very first try and took a sip, only grimacing a little. She rewarded him with a smile.

Finn picked up a glass but didn't drink, she noted. "We'll start near Drumcliffe. It backtracks us, but that was the last place the trace was strong."

"I still do not understand why we do not simply go to Benbulben." Bat had been arguing for that since the afternoon, but each time she was overruled.

"Because, as I have said, the only visions you have seen of the area were of the past, or of Ailis fighting the baobhan sith. There were no signs of the blade, or of Grainne." Finn raised a brow. "Unless there is something you have yet to tell us?"

Did he suspect? If she spoke of her vision of him and Grainne, would that push them in the correct direction? Or would it ensure an outcome that would harm all of them? Instinct continued to hold her words and told her that this particular scene was meant only for her to see, not to tell.

They would end up at Benbulben soon, one way or the other.

~

DUB

He stood behind the bar in his usual place, keeping an eye on Bat. She had asked to help serve for a while, to get used to her new skill.

It was a good strategy, for more than just learning the art of the pint. It told anyone watching that things were fine, that life was moving on, that he wasn't worried, and neither was the goddess.

He had debated keeping the pub closed tonight, but that would be sending the wrong message to the fae of the area and might send some of them running to the more fearsome of the solitary, out of their own belief that dark times were back.

There would be grumbles from some, of course, that they weren't doing enough, that the guardi wouldn't solve this, that they didn't like how the investigation was being handled, things of that nature. But there were always grumbles. If the O'Loinsigh brothers, who were known to keep out of the machinations of the gods and the various tuath, were seen being drawn in, it could create worse than mere grumblings.

They'd opened late. He'd announced this would be the

case for the next week, to allow the goddess and Shar to recover. There had been no keeping either attack quiet, not with this lot.

There was another advantage to remaining open, more important than the other reasons. The gossip.

Mell sat in one of the booths, surrounded by banshee. They'd come in with Meera, nearly buzzing. One leaned in to whisper in his brother's ear and then giggled. Mell flashed his smile, the one that had drawn more than one sigh from a woman over the years.

A splash of beer hit his hand. He twisted and grasped Bat's hand where it pulled down the tap. She'd pulled too hard, sending the pint to overflowing and ruining it. She tore her gaze from the banshee booth and blushed, allowing him to take the glass from her and accepting the rag he handed her without protest.

That was another thing that needed to be addressed. He had not missed the way his brothers watched the goddess, the way Shar pulled her to him, sought her with his gaze, or had hovered until Dub sent him off to fetch more whiskey from storage. He'd be back any moment, a self-appointed shadow for Bat.

Dub would have thought it something to do with how she'd healed his brother's soul, but he'd been doing it even before the incident last night. And Mell, well, he was a little subtler, but he didn't want to imagine what his middle brother may do when the goddess went home.

What will I do when she leaves? Because she would. His body tightened, every muscle bunching in protest to the idea. He nearly smiled as that tightening moved lower. She did this to him, from the first sight of her star-filled eyes. Mixed him up until he was as lost as a wisp's victim in the bog.

Carefully, he placed the ruined pint in the sink behind them. Then he handed Bat another glass and gestured to the tap. She bit her lip and nodded.

A dark chuckle came from farther down the bar. The Far Gorta—the hungry man—who had bothered his goddess the night before was back, tracking her with its gaze. Heat, the familiar warmth of fury, filled him. Dub shifted until he stood directly across the bar from the fae. "Something funny?"

Dark eyes focused on him. "Yes. The O'Loinsigh brothers are about to be brought down. I find it very funny."

Dub didn't need to ask what he meant. He leaned in. "You stay away from her."

The Far Gorta twisted his head to gaze at Bat once more as she placed a nearly perfect pint in front of Darrig. She flashed the leprechaun a small smile when he sipped then raised the pint in acknowledgment of a good drink. The patrons had been very patient tonight.

"I mean it, fae. I can't kill you, but I can certainly make you hurt." Dub reached out with one finger and pushed, sending the fae tumbling off his stool and into the empty table behind him.

"Dub." Bat rushed to him, reproach clear in her thinned lips and drawn brows. She looked at the fallen fae. "Are you all right?"

The Far Gorta rose, brushing off and straightening his already soiled clothing. "I am just fine, goddess." He

223

raised a brow and tilted his head. "I am not the one ya need to be worryin' about, warrior."

Shar appeared beside him. "Leave."

"I thought all were welcome here, giant."

"Not if they're going to be stirring up trouble."

The Far Gorta raised his hands. "Just a bit of teasing never hurt."

Bat raised a finger and shook it, like a mother at her unruly child. "No, you meant mischief and not the fun kind."

The fae raised his hands in surrender. "If I promise not ta tease? Can I stay? It's dark times out there."

His goddess's expression eased. "For now. But if you go out of line again, Dub will throw you out." She demonstrated, pantomiming picking something up and heaving it away. "Just like that."

"I will be good, goddess, I promise. Will ya be playing tonight?"

Dub held himself back as she narrowed her eyes on the fae. "Are you trying to make another deal? No deals."

"No deals," the Far Gorta agreed. "Just a question." Something that may have been true eagerness flitted across the solitary fae's expression. "It's been long since I heard the Uaithne played and played well."

Shar slid past him and placed his hands on Bat's waist, lifting her up and out of the way. "Why don't you take a break and play for a bit?"

Movement near the door caught Dub's eye, a face he hadn't seen in nearly six centuries. "No. I'd like her to get a little more practice, and I need to handle something."

The figure slipped out the door, shadows flowing and

helping to obscure him from sight. Dub put on a bit of speed to catch him.

"Scath." Dub put a bit of his strength behind the summons, though his power did not really work in such a way. But he was his father's eldest, and Scath must at least recognize that power.

A figure stepped out of the shadows next to the building. Dark hair to match Dub's own was bound back in a braid, much as Shar preferred to wear his. Scath's eyes were dark pitch to match the shadows that played around his feet like eager hounds. His father's best spy and assassin hadn't changed. "Dub."

"Why are you here?"

"There have been rumors and whispers, of course. There would be no other reason for me to be any place."

Dub sighed, reminded once again why he preferred to stay out of things. All the damned cryptic references. *Which is just what we have been doing to the goddess.* "Why are you here?" he asked again.

Scath shifted, and those shadows swirled. Dub growled a warning. "Your father sent me," the other man finally said.

Which was also obvious. Scath didn't do anything which his father did not order. Dub waited.

Scath's lips thinned. "The brooch."

And there it was. Shar was right, he and Mell were fools. Damned effing fools that would be better off prancing about the back lanes with bells on their shoes and in their hair, begging to be disemboweled by a bomen. "You know my Da lost it near a millennia ago." And most of his power along with it. A man's brooch was his sign, his honor, and his status made real. For Alatrom to have lost his, and he the leader of the clan, had sunk the O'Loinsighs into near obscurity among the Fomoiri.

"And the rumors I'm following tell me it may have surfaced."

Dub hesitated. This was what they'd wanted, right? To find the brooch and offer it up in return for full freedom from the clan? For true and acknowledged independence, not just the deliberate negligence their father had shown them all these years?

But now there was a new complication. His father was just the type of man to use a nearly powerless goddess to his advantage. Or try to. That she was Egyptian... well, if his father could get some vengeance for his ancestors in the midst of it, all the better.

"Set up a meeting. Three months from now." Bat would be gone, beyond the reach of his father. "And do not think to try to retrieve it before them. The fact that I now hold that chunk of gold gives me an advantage before the Tribunal, as Da well knows. And more than just I know that I hold it. Make that clear to him as well."

Scath bowed his head in acknowledgment and then was gone.

Dub stretched his neck and took a moment to gather his composure. It wouldn't do to enter the pub and strike that Far Gorta again, not after Bat had all but given the thing sanctuary.

He pulled open the door and paused on the threshold. A fire had been lit in the hearth across the room, and Mell had taken up his guitar. Bat leaned against the bar, her eyes closed in enjoyment of the carefully picked melody flowing from his brother's fingers, and Shar hovered beside her. The patrons sipped their pints and whiskeys and nibbled on the few snacks the pub had started offering recently. A laugh rang out from the booth of banshees. There were even a few humans at a table near the fire, uncaring that magic surrounded them. Ailis came in from the kitchen, holding a small plate of cheese and sausages, taking them to the banshees. Finn had taken a stool near the door and sipped a slightly cloudy pint, keeping his sharp gaze focused on the patrons.

It was a good scene. And Dub couldn't imagine it without the dark-haired goddess at the center.

FINN

He watched as Mell ushered the last patron out, a tipsy pixie, and locked the door. Finally, the evening was done and they could get to the business of sorting through what they'd learned tonight. He pulled up a mental map of the area. Benbulben was at most thirty minutes from Sligo. Carney was fifteen and Drumcliffe a mere ten, depending on the traffic. Bat insisted that Benbulben was where they needed to go, but everything she'd told him pointed to her visions being of the past. She'd even admitted at one point to not having a specific vision of Grainne in the present.

Which meant his former love—no, fiancée, she'd never really been his love, he needed to remember that—could be anywhere.

227

Hopefully, someone had heard something useful tonight. Otherwise, they would return to systematically scanning and tracing. And while they would not need to search the whole of Ireland, Grainne had always been skilled with glamour. It was why it had taken so long to find her and Diarmuid in the first place. The only way he'd been able to trace them in the end was by following the blank spots, the areas where there was nothing to find surrounded by the unease of other fae.

That was what he'd found in Carney. Drumcliffe also had patches of blank. It was quite possible there were other trails to follow, ones that lead in a different direction than Carney. To Benbulben even.

Resentment stirred, closing his throat. It was childish of him, he knew, but he did not want to follow the lead of this goddess, who had nothing to her, yet dared call him a coward. What burned the most was that none of the others in the room had objected to her statement.

And he couldn't either, for she had been correct.

Ailis and Shar were seated in stools next to him at the bar. Bat and Dub were across from them, cleaning up behind the bar. Mell slid in beside them and started on drying the glasses as Bat rinsed. Finn barely held his sneer. A goddess who did dishes. *Grainne would never have—*

He cut off the thought. Already it started. He hadn't even seen her, and Grainne pulled him into old ways of thinking. She was a fae, nothing more, and yet he'd just compared her to a true goddess, and found the deity lacking. When in reality, Bat was more than Grainne had ever been in so many ways.

Was it possible to both love and hate someone at the same time?

Bat handed a dish to Mell and then half turned, her gaze, both dark and shining with millions of lights, trained on him as though she heard his thoughts. Was that also a power of hers? *...there are many kinds of beauty in this world, just as there are many forms of darkness...*

"The banshees said there's some talk of the bomen in the trees around Benbulben being frightened of something," he started, leading with the piece of information that may please Bat. "Not much frightens the bomen. Then again, it could simply be a stray cat. Bomen are not much fond of felines."

She inclined her head and turned back to the dishes. What was she thinking?

"And the pixies were saying the tracks around Derryfad had traces of glamour," Mell added.

That was only a few minutes north of Carney. Finn glanced at this phone, double-checking the message that had come in about an hour ago. "Oisin reported an incident with the selkies, but I doubt Grainne would have gone all the way out there."

"Con called earlier." Ailis leaned forward. "Ya remember him, he was with me the night we met?" she asked Bat, who nodded. "He was talking about a group of hikers in the Gortarowey who got lost and ended up in hospital. Faint. Doctors said it was dehydration."

"Coulda been the baobhan sith," Mell said, and Finn nodded. The Gortarowey also wasn't far from Benbulben. Was he foolish in ignoring Bat's words of Benbulben? She had not insisted too strongly and had not offered any additional insights through her visions. The rest had also followed his lead. Or had they followed her lead when she relented?

He shook off the doubts. He had done this before and very successfully. He would keep Bat with him, as it seemed her senses pierced the glamour Grainne could pull around herself, even if it was at a very short range. Besides, if they went to Benbulben, at most he may gain a trace unless Grainne was there at the very moment they arrived.

"Anyone else?" Finn asked. When no one spoke up, he said, "Then we stick with the original plan for now and go to Drumcliffe." The guardi pinned a look on Bat when her lips thinned. "I know you think we need to go to Benbulben, but I have tracked many, many things in my existence. I do trust your visions, goddess, but without a confirmation of the when of what you have seen, it would be a waste to go there unless we are sure of her presence at that time."

Bat tilted her head, those eyes of her stripping away the layers of justification and doubt and reasoning and, yes, fear, that crowded around him. Then she nodded and returned to her dishes once more.

Dub shifted, pressing his arm to Bat's in a deliberate movement.

Finn wondered what the goddess would do once she realized she'd been claimed. Despite what they may be telling her, or themselves, they were not going to let her go so easily when the lease ran out on that apartment.

~

MELL

It took much for him not to lean down and kiss his goddess goodnight at her door. But Ailis and his brothers stood right there.

Plus, there was a reluctance there, a... doubt, when she looked at him or his brothers. There was also doubt of Finn, but it was different. She didn't trust the guardi to do what was needed with Grainne when it came time.

It wasn't anything they had discussed yet, but there was only one sentence the Tribunal offered for the crime of using a *lann de anam* against an innocent, and that was to die by the same fate you had bestowed upon others. It was a bit "eye for an eye" for his tastes, but as Dub once said, sometimes evil had to be stopped.

The doubt Bat held for Mell and his brothers was similar. She didn't trust them, but not in regards Grainne. No, this doubt was subtler, and he wasn't sure if she or anyone else was even aware of it.

She didn't trust them to *stay*. She didn't trust anyone to stay.

He wanted to reach into her, to heal the old wounds left by the other deities of her land. He wanted to find the holes of her soul and patch them, just as she had with Shar. For as surely as the blade had ripped his brother's spirit, and would have eventually bled his vitality away, the wounds in his goddess's being were just as deadly in other ways.

Even if, as she said, she couldn't die.

"Mell." Dub stood at the end of the hall outside the door to their office, warning frown pulling his lips down.

Mell realized he still stared at Bat's door. He drew in a breath and let it out, slowly, carefully. He didn't want to set off the grumpy Fomoiri. Dub was on the verge of going off, and there was no Egyptian goddess in the hallway to kiss and diffuse the situation.

And hadn't that little incident been telling? Mell knew why his brother had been so angry. But Dub had misinterpreted the pain, and yes disgust, that had crowded in on Mell. It had been *for* his goddess, not because of her. When she had, once again, stated she was a goddess, it had hit him just how far she had fallen. She felt so close to human. Even the least of the deities in Eire weren't so low as that. And he knew that immortals and gods alike would take one look at her and assume the worst, that she was low.

But she was not. All she needed was... a little care. He —no, *they*—could be the ones to give it to her.

Because it had also not been lost on him that she felt an attraction to all of them. Probably one of the worst things they could do for her would be to pursue her and then force her to make a decision she was not ready to make. It would backfire, and they'd lose her altogether.

"Mell." Dub's voice, though quiet, ripped through his thoughts.

"Right. What, brother?"

"We have some things we need to discuss. Tonight."

Shar, who had rounded the stairs and crossed to his side of the hall, drew to a halt. His gaze darted from Dub to Mell to Bat's door then back to Dub. He nodded.

Mell sighed. Yes, there were things they needed to

speak of, but he wasn't sure his brothers were thinking of the same things he was.

They'd turned one of the larger bedrooms into their office. It wasn't much, but there was space for three desks, shelves, cabinets, and three very large bodies. They'd also splurged on the fancy chairs from the store, the ones covered in leather and that a body could take a nap in if they weren't careful. Mell had definitely had a few of those naps.

Mell plopped into his and spun around, facing his brothers. Family meeting time. They'd been having more and more of these over the decades, as though Dub was afraid he and Shar would run screaming into the fields, stripped naked and flailing arms and swords and spears, oh my.

None of them spoke. That was strange. Dub usually got right to the point.

"We can't pursue the goddess."

"I asked her to stay."

"Scath was here tonight."

They all spoke at once, but Dub won. Mell jerked and Shar stilled.

"Da's heard about the brooch," Shar guessed.

"Yes. This was not how we planned to approach this—"

Shar stood, looming over his two brothers. Mell half expected him to grab the backs of his and Dub's heads and knock them together. "And how did you plan to approach this? What possible outcome could you be seeking by taunting Da with the O'Loinsigh brooch?"

Dub tilted his head back. "Our freedom to begin our own clan."

That shut Shar up and quickly. "Oh."

"Scath saw Bat tonight. No doubt he'll be telling Da about her as well. I told him to set up a meeting for three months from now. That should keep the goddess out of any of Da's machinations. She'll be home by then." Dub rubbed a hand over his face, and Mell could sense the struggle in him. His brother didn't want the goddess gone, but he did want her away from their father and the rest of the Fomoiri.

A rush of adrenaline caught Mell in its grip as his anger surged forward. He didn't try to keep it from his brothers, and they both flinched. "Well, ya've both fucked us. Ya've fucked the goddess as well. Shar asks her to stay, Dub sets up meetings with immortals who'd tear her apart given a chance, and neither one of ya even thinking of what this will do to her. Do ya even comprehend what she's been through? How much courage it took for her to come here? And what will happen if we go to her and ask her to leave after Shar asked her to stay?" Mell rose, his fists clenched. He wanted to strike out, hit them, make them bleed. "Ya'r idjits, both of ya. I'm ashamed, I am, to call ya family."

Dub's lips tightened, and a wave of fury came from him. Mell braced for the attack.

"What did they do to her?" His brother's voice was low, barely contained.

Mell's attention sharpened. "No' what ye're thinking." He swallowed, struggling to bring his own emotions under control. "But imagine being ignored and dismissed, and left, for millennia. Not just the humans, but the other gods themselves. There such a sense of... isolation around her. I mean, did ya see the way she reacted to a pair of boots? A bowl of strawberries? And when," he said, pointing at Dub. "Ya so casually threw out 'what ya care to give' at her, she damn near fell into love with ya. She keeps saying she can't be killed, but under that, I wonder if she doesn't wish for it."

Shar stared with wide eyes at the wall. Remorse and something close to grief radiated from his brother. "I didn't know."

Mell threw up his hands. "How did ya think she got as she is? And of course, you didn't know. Ya see a girl who walks into a pub like she owns the place, picks up the damn harp, and sits there like a regal queen before her subjects. She doesn't even know, or she doesn't acknowledge it. She sits there thinking of home and comfort and hope and... she doesn't believe in it. She wants it, but she doesn't believe."

Shar's hands curled into fists and straightened out, curled and straightened. "It's easier to fight for others than it is for yourself," he whispered. "She's so fierce about Dano and finding Grainne and the blade."

"We can't send her away." Dub straightened and stood. Pacing three feet in one direction he spun and paced back.

"Sit back down," Mell said from his chair. "This office isn't big enough for that." He shot a look at Shar, who slowly sank into his own seat once more.

Dub glared, but also dropped into his chair. "Can't send her away, but I don't want her involved in this business with Da."

"It's got to be her decision," Shar grumbled. "If she decides to go, we can't keep her."

"The hell we can't," Dub ground out.

Mell nearly laughed. His earlier anger had evaporated in the face of his brothers' reactions to his words, and Dub's very quick about-face was mirth worthy. And more than ironic.

"Agreed." Both brothers glared at him. "We will not send her away, nor will we make her stay. But we can do all in our power to convince her to stay." He drew in a breath and braced himself. He really had no idea how his next statement would go over. "I want her. And so do you." He pointed first at Shar, then at Dub. "That will be a problem."

Shar nodded. "She has already said she worries of upsetting the balance between us."

"So, what, we compete for her? The brehons still recognize a willing kidnapping..." Dub's lips quirked, and his anger leached away.

Interesting.

Both brothers looked to Mell, the one who could see into the emotions of their guest. "She is attracted to us all," he admitted. "*My* fear is that she will hold off on taking any action for fear of our reactions and losing us all. We need to build her trust in us, show her that we are not going anywhere, no matter what she chooses." He put on his stern face. "Which means we need to be sure of our reactions, whether she chooses one of us, none of us, someone else..." *Or all of us.* But he didn't say the last out loud.

Dub wore his contemplative frown, and Shar rocked in his seat.

"She has said she would think about things after Grainne has been apprehended and the blade recovered," Shar said. "I suggest we do the same thing." He rolled his shoulders. "I want her near, no matter the form it takes. But I will not lie and say I do not want more, all of her. If she chooses another…" his fists clenched and pressed into his knees. "I do not know how I will truly react. I will need to think on this."

"No going outside unaccompanied," Dub cut in.

Mell knew his younger brother would have headed directly for the garden usually. He himself would need to find a quiet and abandoned corner of some field to sort through what were his own emotions and what was bleeding through from his brothers. And Dub… well, his oldest brother would head for the old forge he kept hidden a few miles to the south.

Until it was safe to do those things, they'd just have to wait and deal with it.

"Hah," Mell said, realizing something. "I just acted as a proper middle brother, didn't I? Getting you two out of the trouble you'd set for yourselves and mediating the meeting." He sent them proper middle-brother-smirks. "But for now, we are agreed. We do want her to stay, in some form." He waited as they nodded again, confirming. "The rest we will decide upon and sort out later."

Chapter Twenty-Two

Dearest Bastet,
Men are annoying. They always have been, and they always
will be. I think it is inherent.

- Bat, the frustrated goddess

BAT

*B*at breathed out in one long breath and relaxed her shoulders. The time was coming.

Finn was here, in the pub, debating with the brothers on whether they should search for traces to the east or the west of Drumcliffe first.

She'd had another flash last night, just before Ailis turned out the lights.

Flash. Her and Ailis in a small bubble of a car, speeding toward Benbulben.

It came again. And the very real and urgent sense of now accompanied that flash. Though Bat had never been able to pinpoint the exact times her visions would take place, she knew the final confrontation with Grainne was drawing near. If they could get there at the proper moment.

She glanced to where the men had gathered at the bar, three dark heads and one of light red bent together. Hushed and harsh voices resounded through the room. The brothers were in a mood this morning, and Finn was as stubborn as ever.

Ailis moved next to her and crossed her arms, her gaze also on the men. After a moment she snorted. "Do you want to just take my car out to Benbulben?"

The question was so casual, so smoothly uttered, that Bat didn't react right away. Could Ailis read more than emotions? "Leave them here?"

Ailis nodded. "They'll just end up getting in the way."

Bat thought about it, she really did. Across the room Dub stiffened and shook his head while Shar crossed his arms and frowned. Finn, his back to her, gestured widely. Mell, usually the most expressive, was locked down. She couldn't get anything from him, which meant whatever they were discussing, he didn't like.

"I think we're going to need them, unfortunately. Some of my visions... If we're going to make it through this, all of us will need to be there." Raised voices interrupted her, though she couldn't understand the words. They must have slipped into one of the old dialects. "Can you tell what they are saying?"

Tilting her head, Ailis concentrated. "It is muffled, but I think they are arguing about whether or not to leave you out, like bait. Maybe draw her out. And... whether to go after the sith first."

"We are back to that? Is the sith really a problem?"

"During the day? No. Honestly, they don't leave their territory often these days. If Grainne is eliminated, the sith will probably return home on her own. Unless she's truly been adopted by them, in which case there may be retaliation." Ailis grinned and bounced on her feet.

Bat twisted her head around to watch her. "So, you like a little retribution?"

"Oh, always. It's been way too boring around here."

Turning back to the men, who were still going strong, the corner of her mouth curled into a grin. "When this is done, I have a goddess to introduce you to. I think the two of you would get along like..."

"Two cats in a sack?"

Bat couldn't hold back her crack of laughter. "Something like that." She crossed her own arms, matching Ailis. "They will never agree, will they?"

"Probably not."

"I think we *should* take your car."

Ailis straightened up. "Perfect. I'll go get it. Maybe ten minutes? I'll bring it 'round the back." She shot a quick look at the men. "Just you get away."

Oh, she would, she would. For things to progress, they had to leave the damned pub. Bat nodded and Ailis strolled to the front door, unlocked it, and strolled out. By the time the others knew what she was doing, she was gone.

"Dammit, Ailis, you can't just walk around alone." Finn stood in the door calling out after her.

Whatever the green haired woman did next had Finn's fingers going white against the doorknob. He stepped back and slammed the door closed then spun to face Bat. "What are you two up to?" He advanced on her, face tight with anger. "What ridiculous plan have you concocted?"

Bat bristled. How dare he? "Maybe she just got tired of you... dithering?" She dropped her arms and braced her legs. She was not a goddess of war, but she knew a few things. She could probably remember them in time to kick this not-man's ass, as Bastet—and Ailis—would say.

A broad back appeared in front of her. Shar had slipped between them. "Do not."

Bat poked her head around him to see Dub and Mell on either side of Finn, fists clenched and eyes locked on the guardi.

To intervene or not? "I'm going to the kitchen. I would like to try to make the tea for myself. If you will excuse me, I will leave you men to your... planning." Bat slid from behind Shar and strode for the kitchen, not looking back. There was a scuff, the sound of wood hitting wood, and low words, but it didn't seem any real violence was going to erupt.

Shame.

And you are letting Ailis rub off on you.

She filled the kettle and banged a few cabinet doors. There was no tin of bags in sight. She didn't actually know where the tea was kept; she'd have to get Shar to show her. Later. Pausing, she stood just out of sight of the pub common room and listened. They were still at it. She found a pad and pen in one of the drawers near the cupboard and wrote a quick note.

Meet us at Benbulben.
- Bat
p.s. – arguing is a waste of time.

She tucked the note under a mug and moved to the back door. Hand on the doorknob, she paused. Was she doing the right thing? It felt wrong to leave the brothers behind. Their hesitation, however, and inability to agree on a plan of action, was going to ensure that Grainne either succeeded in her plans or escaped justice yet again. The sense of urgency welled in her chest, and she yanked the door open. A small car, green of course, idled at the edge of the alley and Bat hurried to it.

Ailis glanced over as Bat slid into the passenger seat. "Ready?"

Bat twisted, sending one last look at the pub. "As I will ever be." As they pulled out into the main street, she murmured, "Hope they find the note soon."

DUB

She'd been gone too long.

Finn was still going on about the baobhan sith. He kept arguing that if they could find her, the creature would lead them to Grainne. Except his logic was faulty because they already had someone who could lead them to the devil-woman. Finn had never been logical when it came to Grainne, though. Never. And that woman was poison, always had been, always would be. It was as though Finn couldn't see it. Even now…

"I'm telling you, the baobhan sith will lead us to the dagger. I should be trying to get her trace. They're probably just using Grainne. And how do we really know what your goddess felt was Grainne and not the blade, or the sith?" Finn said. It was as though all the progress they'd made with him had disappeared overnight.

Dub shifted on his feet, restless, as his brothers argued with the guardi. The guardi who was levelheaded and hard as nails on any other subject.

"How long does it take to make tea?" Dub, not waiting for an answer, strode for the kitchen.

It was empty.

He slammed a hand against the wall beside the door. "Gods dammit." Then he spied a scrap of paper under a mug. Snatching it up, he braced himself—for either a ransom note or confirmation that their goddess had taken matters into her own hands.

"Where is she?" Shar asked from the doorway, Mell and Finn crowded behind him in the hall.

"Benbulben. She and Ailis went off to Benbulben on their own." He crumpled the note in his fist. Grabbing the keys from their place on a hook near the trim, he yanked open the back door. Borrowing Bat's words, he called out, "Arguing is a waste of time."

The others scrambled behind him, echoes of curses

ringing in his ears. "Wait," Shar said, halting on the back stoop. "Do you have...?"

"Of course. Get in."

Did Dub have his sword? No matter how many years went by, he never left home without it. What did his brother think of him? At times it had been his closest companion, folded in a pocket of space, and never far from him. A trick his father taught him, and that he had in turn shown his brothers. There had been *one* time he left it behind, a feast at a country castle near Lough Conn—the castle long since destroyed—and Shar never let him forget.

He traced a quick rune of hiding and pulled out onto the main street. Pressing his foot on the gas, he sped through the roads, only twice needing to swerve to avoid pedestrians.

"Did you...?"

This time it was Mell asking and Dub hit the steering wheel. "What do you take me for? Of course, I did."

"It's just that one time—"

"I set the damn ward." He knew his brothers were simply anxious—terrified more like—and restless at having to sit in a rusted old truck while their goddess was in who knew what trouble already, but couldn't they have a little faith?

He flicked a look in the rearview mirror, studying Finn. He was going to be the variable in this. The de Danann sat in tense silence, his gaze unfocused. Old memories flashed through Dub's mind. The last time he'd been to that cursed mountain, he'd slain an immortal. He didn't regret the action itself, only the necessity of it. "Diarmuid was a good man." The words slipped from him and his stomach tightened. Diarmuid *had* been a good man, before...

"Before Grainne, you mean." Finn's lips barely moved as he spoke.

Dub held his silence. Yes, he meant before Grainne. As one trained in the ways of the Druid, and the Brehon, he was well versed in the law. Diarmuid had always abided, always respected the order of the universe, until that woman came along.

For a time, she had held all the Fianna under her spell. As the soon-to-be wife of their leader, Finn, she had been idolized, exalted, celebrated. Even he had taken to calling her by the name of Bandia, naming her a goddess that she was not.

Then, one night, under a moon that glowed down with silver, turning the countryside into a place he imagined resembled the Otherlands, he had seen her pressed against Mell, her hand tracing a path along his thigh. Mell's emotions screamed out of him, a mixture of desire, lust, fear, and anger. There was even a splash of repugnance. Dub's emotions had been confused: anger that Mell would betray Finn that way and jealousy that he himself had not been chosen. It was a dark moment for him, one of the darkest of his life. His hand had crept to his dagger and clasped the hilt. He had been ready to attack his own brother.

Then Mell had gripped the woman's hand, pushed it away, and said one word. "No."

It broke her spell, and Dub's mind had cleared. He'd stepped up beside them, making his presence known.

Though he didn't say anything, Grainne's eyes had narrowed on him, promising retribution if he, or Mell, breathed a word.

They never had. And it cracked whatever bond he'd felt for his then leader, a man that—despite Dub's heritage and upbringing—he had respected as honorable and just.

Months later Grainne disappeared with Diarmuid, setting in motion events that led to the loss of too many innocents, and a battle on the fields below Benbulben.

His left eyelid twitched. "I'm sorry," he said now. He kept his eyes on the road, his hands steady on the wheel as he pressed the accelerator, taking them up to speeds the truck was never meant to handle. The shudder of the overworked engine had the vehicle shaking right along with it, vibrating through his bones. He continued, needing to get the words out. "We should have told you. Mell and I, we should have told you what she was doing. With the men. But... you were so happy to have her as yours, and I... did not trust your reaction. She had a way about her." He finished, knowing it was a paltry excuse, but it was all he had.

"I always knew what she was," Mell said. His words carried a hint of defiance. "How the rest of you couldn't see it, I'll never know."

In the passenger seat, Shar turned his head and looked out the side window. Even he, though not of the Fianna at that time, had been affected by this period of their past. He had been given the honor of guarding the Rowan—the tree that protected them all—by Dana herself. His brother didn't talk about it much, but he knew Grainne had tricked him, allowing Diarmuid to gain access to the berries and destroy the tree.

Silence, thick as the clouds that had rolled in above them, fell over the cab of the truck.

Dub almost missed it. The damn turnoff wasn't marked, and it had been too long since he came this way. He slammed onto the brakes, sending the truck into a skid before they came to a stop, the right half of the truck coming off the road.

"Fuck, man, get it together," Mell ground out, his arm braced against the door.

Dub threw the truck in reverse, quickly backing up and turning onto the narrow lane.

They were almost there. *Almost there, almost there*. He chanted the words as a light mist started falling, obscuring his view. He flipped on the wipers just as Ailis's little green car came into view, parked on the narrow shoulder. He ground to halt, the tires kicking up damp gravel and gouging shallow ruts in the grass. Jumping out, he surveyed the low hills, the pink of early spring flowers standing out in clumps. Benbulben towered over them, the wrinkled upper slopes like a hag's lips, but so green they pierced his soul.

And, he didn't see her.

"Fuck, we need a way to track her after this," Shar mumbled from beside him.

If there was an "after this." Dub pushed away the thought. Now was not the time. "Mell?"

"Already on it." Mell closed his eyes and his lips thinned.

"Now is the time, Finn," Dub said.

The guardi nodded. Taking a deep breath, he held it in. "I could be off."

Dub growled. "Just tell us which way."

Finn pointed. Toward Benbulben, and to the far corner. Mell nodded, confirming.

Fine then.

Dub took off, putting his strength into his legs, transforming it into speed. What would take the others a precious ten minutes took him two. He rounded the far end of the mountain, one of the extensions that gave it the shape of a jaw, and sucked in a breath.

The first person he saw was Ailis, crouched before a brown-haired creature in a flowing and ragged green dress. The baobhan sith. They circled each other slowly, Ailis holding a dagger, the blade tipped in red. As she continued to move, he saw that one side of her head was drenched in blood. She bared her teeth and lunged, catching the sith with the tip of the dagger and then jumping out of reach of the clawing hands.

Ailis was doing fine. *Now, where...*

There she stood, his goddess, her dark hair blowing about in damp strands. Her pink sweater was too big, her tights clashed with her boots, and there was a stain on one thigh. He hopped it wasn't blood. Opposite her stood a woman who at one point had been the dream of many men.

The only thing still beautiful about Grainne was her hair, a red gold that shone even in the rain. In reality, she looked the same as she always had, the lovely exterior that held the heart of a serpent. Now, though, her skin looked too pale, her eyes not dark enough, and her face lacked the graceful roundness of his goddess.

In her hand was clutched a dagger glowing with a dark light.

As he took his first step toward them, Grainne lashed out, much as Ailis had done with the vampire. He put all of his strength into his next strides, even as his goddess stumbled back, clutching her side.

But, she didn't fall. And in the next moments, Dub saw exactly why she was a goddess.

Chapter Twenty-Three

Bastet,
I'm wondering if I should tell you...
But it does not seem to be my secret to tell.
- Bat

BAT

*B*at clasped her hands over the new wound. Unlike the gunshot, this one didn't bleed as much. Nor did it have the same shock factor.

Instead, it nicked her essence, and a piece of her fell away. The blade sucked it up. Bat could feel it now, just what this blade was. It was a... repository. The small part of her that it held showed her the other souls it kept captive. There was the little girl from her vision, and there was Diarmuid, his golden hair shining. He smiled at her with an appealing innocence that was in stark contrast to how she had seen him in her vision. Behind him stood others, men, women, some beautiful and slim, some shorter, and dark. She searched, but only saw those two familiar faces.

Then she spotted him. Dano. He smiled at her, his red hair messy, and gave her a little bow.

None of these spirits approached her or made any move to communicate. She could sense a little of what remained, mostly feelings of longing and remorse, but all she really felt was peace.

Still... they were trapped in this place, used as the fuel for the magic of those who would use the blade. She reached out, seeking the connection that kept them bound. It eluded her, but in her search, she saw something new.

The blade itself was not an evil thing.

She had suspected as much, since she had only really ever sensed Grainne's wickedness, never the blade's. Now she could confirm it. In the distance, hidden behind rows of stolen souls, was a line of shadows, spirits so long trapped they were almost fully depleted. She could sense the same peace from them, but also purpose. They had *chosen* to enter the blade. Had chosen to give their lives. Because beyond these shadows was something even darker.

The blade was a *prison*.

As she watched, the little girl tilted her head and nodded. Then she turned and walked to the line of shadows, the other spirits parting for her. When she reached that line, one of the shadows held out its hand and the girl took it. She joined the line, her colors dimming as her energy joined the others... holding back that darkness.

I need to be firmer in my questions on these soul blades when this is all done.

Her attention returned to Dano and she held out her hand to him. He eyed it and slowly stretched out his own. When his palm should have met hers, though, it passed right through. Her fingers curled in and she smiled at him, a promise that she would be back. For hadn't she also promised to gather the pieces of his soul and allow him a place in the Otherworld?

She pulled her consciousness back from the blade and smiled at Grainne. "You have no idea what you are dealing with, do you?"

The woman's eyes narrowed. She really was beautiful, as the men had said. She would have easily been worshipped in Egypt—if she had been a true goddess. But you could not change your essence, your very fabric. This not-woman of the red-gold hair would only ever be that, a not-woman of finite power.

Bat spread her arms and revealed her own essence to this woman.

No, she did not have much power. But a goddess was still a goddess. She opened her mind's eye and called to the stars above, to Sky Mother and Earth Father, not as a supplicant but as an equal. They filled her, lending her their power for this moment. Keeping her eyes locked on Grainne, Bat turned her hands until her palms faced up, and small swirls of light danced there. She opened her mouth, and words flowed from her.

"She of the two faces, who has chosen. For she has saved herself from evil."

The sound echoed with the force of thunder above the red lands, with the power of Seth and Shu and Gub; with the music of three thousand stars, and the caress of Nut and Isis. And Bat remembered her creation, and the choice she had made. For in that choice was her salvation.

She flicked her fingers at the figure that now huddled before her.

"No!"

A body slammed into her, just as another brought down Grainne. The power she held shot out, flying up into the sky. Whoever had her twisted in mid-air so that when they hit the ground she was cushioned by a solid bulk. Lapis eyes stared up at her, brows drawn together in a frown.

"Dub?"

"You are the most stubborn woman—goddess—agh." Then his mouth slammed down on hers in a hard kiss, more frustration than passion. After a bare second, he pulled back, still frowning. "What were you thinking?"

She opened her mouth to say she knew not what, when something slammed to the ground beside her. Twisting her head, she saw a large black bird on its back, wings twisted and legs curled in. It didn't move.

"Fuck." Mell stood over them staring at the bird. "You had to go and kill one of the Morrigan's messengers, didn't you?"

What? What was he talking about? She hadn't killed anything? Then she recalled the power that she had gathered and its wayward trajectory. "I'm blaming Dub for that." Though, this creature didn't deserve to die.

The power was mostly gone, but Sky and Earth lingered in her, Earth holding a dark amusement. With a huff, and using the last of what they had shared with her, she repaired the snapped bones and broken feathers. She expanded the small lungs and beat the tiny heart. Then she called upon the Sky Mother one last time, bringing a spark of life to the animal.

It jerked, squawked, and flipped to its feet. Flapping its wings, it snapped at her before taking off and disappearing over the crest of Benbulben.

"Huh. Well, that may fix it." Mell crossed his arms and glared down at her.

Dub's arms tightened around her as she twisted her head to where Grainne had stood a moment ago. This wasn't over, and these brothers may have ruined their best chance of stopping the evil.

The sight that greeted her was the fulfillment of yet another vision, and though it should not have surprised her, shock stole through her limbs. Grainne, with her hair —somehow dry—flowing down her back, gazed up at Finn with pleading eyes that glowed with a green as bright as the hills of this land. Her lips parted prettily, and her delicate hands were clasped at her middle. As Bat watched, those wide eyes filled with tears and her lips trembled in a way that almost fooled even Bat.

"Please. Please don't." Her voice was soft, entrancing, and Bat heard echoes of power in it.

Seduction. The fae's power was that of seduction.

Finn gripped the knife, a tremor, barely seen, making the blade seem blurry and insubstantial.

"Please." Grainne bit her lip. "You loved me once."

Finn's hand lowered minutely.

A cry rang out from across the field. Ailis. Bat pushed away from Dub's chest and twisted in the direction she'd last seen her friend. The baobhan sith lay on the ground, Ailis crouched over her holding her blade to the fae's throat while Shar... sat on her? Okay then.

Bat twisted back to Finn and Grainne, still propped up on top of Dub. She couldn't see his face, but the trembling had stopped, and his hand was steady. His chest expanded with a deep breath, and as he let it out, his shoulders pulled back.

"Grainne, daughter of Cormac." Finn's voice rang out, carrying over the land. The wind stilled and even the misting rain paused. "You are here, before us, accused of the crimes of murder and the use of a soul blade. In addition, you have corrupted your fellow fae to follow you on this path. Payment is required. How will you pay?"

The words were rote, a ritual enacted when the outcome was already assured.

"My family will pay, as is their duty." Despite the pleading look on her face, her words were cold.

"Your family has repudiated you. Long ago, they repudiated you."

"And have you, my once fiancé, repudiated me?"

Flash. Grainne, the life fading from her green eyes, pale skin ashen, as a fine mist fell on a field of green.

Finn nodded. "I have. As you know, there is only one true payment for your crime."

The decision was made.

Grainne sucked in a breath as Finn stood steady before her. Bat could do nothing but watch the events unfold. Maybe she could have protested or stopped the next few seconds from happening. But as she had told Finn earlier, he had a decision to make.

And as Dub said, sometimes evil needed to be stopped.

Bat's fingers dug into Dub's chest and he sucked in a breath. She dropped her gaze to his, unwilling to watch the next few seconds. Let the others see this. Let the others observe the will of fate, which not even gods or goddesses could escape. Let them see justice as the universe served it, for deeds of both obvious and more subtle evil. For just as Grainne was guilty of murder and corruption and greed, so was Finn guilty of allowing the woman to get away with it. He knew who and what this woman was. He had always known, and he had a price to pay for that crime.

Let the others bear witness. Bat was going to look into eyes of lapis blue. "It could never end any other way," she whispered to her not-man.

Dub's eyes widened as four cries rang out. One of defiance and madness. One of grief and longing. One of surprise. And one of triumph.

"Woo hoo!" Ailis called out. "Yes! Ding-dong, the bitch is dead. Hah!"

Bat never took her gaze from Dub. "Why did you stop me?"

His eyes narrowed, and his hands came up to grip her sides. "The Morrigan is the justice bringer of these lands. The guardi carry out her will."

"And you didn't want me interfering, again," she said.

He shifted her off him and she lay on her side in the damp grass as a light mist continued to fall. "I didn't want her to have a reason to drive you away," he said.

She rolled onto her back as he stood, then twisted to see Finn, still standing, Grainne's body at his feet. The soul blade's hilt jutted from her lower chest. Bat wondered if these Irish knew what the blade truly was, what all of them were. Idly, she wondered again just how many of these prisons existed.

She could still feel the blade through that small bit of her essence trapped inside. Grainne was in there now, and unlike Diarmuid and the others, she was not at peace. Even as Bat observed this, something about the blade settled over Grainne, and the restless spirit stilled. A red symbol briefly glowed in her mind's eye.

Mell stood beside Finn now, while Dub still looked down at Bat.

"I think you should go be with your friend now," she said. "He is your friend, right?"

Dub's gaze roved over her face and he nodded, stepping back from her.

"Wait."

He paused.

"Help me up? I'm damp again, and I'm getting cold."

He offered her a hand, and a small smile. Just what she'd been going for.

Chapter Twenty-Four

Dear Bastet,

I have a computer now! Actually, Mell is allowing me to use his. He also says he knows what is wrong with my phone and will help me get it fixed.

You'll see a lot of notes from me. But the thing you need to know, is I am happy. Right now, I am so happy in this pub you helped me find. I help behind the bar and play the harp with Mell and other patrons. They call them sing-songs. Isn't that charming?

I'm also getting to know the regulars. That's what they call patrons when they come to the pub almost every day. Regulars. And they all have their seats they claim as though they owned them, and if someone sits in them... well, Dub can be very intimidating if a simple explanation doesn't work to get a stranger to move. I like these immortals. Many of them are forgotten or outcasts, like me. I can give them a bit of hope if visions come to me, or comfort through a song.

I meet humans too, though they do not recognize me, of course. The Morrigan, a local goddess, has said I may stay, as long as there are no sacrifices or large supplications. I can accept offerings, though, and have a small collection forming.

I really do wish you would visit. I know, I know, you will probably say to yourself, "But I will see Bat in a little more than a month." I am thinking, though, that I will stay longer. The brothers… it is not just the brothers, but they all asked me to stay. There was no time limit given. I like that.

Or maybe you will not say that. Maybe you have a bit of the future in you as well and saw more than I could about this place. Or maybe you were your usual mischievous self and decided to throw all these pieces together to see what would happen. Regardless. Thank you. I would not have tried without your encouragement.

I have to go now, it is almost time for us to open. Imagine me, Bat, a pub-keeper. It boggles the mind a little. (This is a new saying I heard. I like it, and the word is fun to say.)

- Bat, a happy goddess

p.s. I got a puppy! Please don't be mad.

BAT

The pub opened in just thirty minutes and she had much to do to prepare.

The last two weeks had been interesting, to say the least. That day out on Benbulben, they'd stayed there for hours. She and Ailis had eventually gone to Ailis' car and sat in it, heater turned on, while the men did whatever men did when a beautiful woman was killed. She was also not too proud to admit she had been gratified that the brothers had paid more attention to Finn and his state than to the woman with a soul blade buried in her.

Even the baobhan sith had seemed more intent on the men than her friend. But, apparently, they were like that.

Then Finn called the Ceilte Guardi, and they had shown up en masse, the Morrigan in her own shiny black SUV. She'd surveyed the scene, spotted the little green car Bat and Ailis still sat in, and strode over. Ailis rolled down the window and the Morrigan bent over until her gaze met Bat's. "Do not think that this excuses you from the restrictions we have laid down." Small lines formed between her brows, the only sign of her displeasure. "And I would appreciate it if you stayed away from my birds in the future."

With that, she had straightened, spun on her heel so her coat flared around her, and strode to the men still huddled around the body. She looked down at the fallen woman, laid a hand on Finn's shoulder, and two seconds later had everyone in motion. The blade was wrapped and handed over to her, the body gathered, the baobhan sith led away to another car, and then everyone headed away from the strange mountain.

After that... life went on, falling into a routine. Ailis stopped by the pub sometimes. Bat would play a tune or two with Mell each night. For breakfast, there were strawberries and whiskey-laced tea. She'd gotten a pair of gloves and two scarfs.

She soaked it up like the red lands soaked up water. Gradually, she was building her strength.

A soft scuff came from the direction of the hall and the brothers filed into the pub.

"Little goddess, we have an offering for you." Shar stepped up to the bar where Bat was wiping down pint glasses. He gave her that soft smile of his, pulling on her heart. Mell stood to his left, rocking back and forth on his heels, almost bouncing. A grin tugged at this mouth and he looked like a mischievous boy who held his secrets only until he could tell them. Dub, on the other side of Shar, didn't smile, but he wasn't frowning either, and the glow of his eyes was softer than she had seen.

A small yip came from behind them, and a little whine. That sounded like...

"A puppy?" Bat bounced on her feet, forgetting for the moment that she would eventually leave. "You got one of the puppies?"

Dub stepped to the side and held up a squirming bundle.

It was the cream colored one, the puppy that had followed her around the yard, and sat in her lap. Its large brown eyes met hers and he whined, his tail wagging, hitting Dub's chest and sides in a frenzy of excitement.

Bat knew just how he felt. "Oh, puppy. Oh, come here." She held out her arms and made eager motions with her hands, like a five-year-old.

Dub didn't release him to her though. "This offering comes with a request."

She stiffened. "That borders on violating my agreement with the Morrigan. I can only grant smaller supplications, and a puppy seems very grand to me. That was the deal with your Morrigan."

Mell laughed. "We won't tell her if you won't."

Raising a brow, she glanced at each of them in turn, their expressions both eager and wary. "What is your request?"

Dub set the puppy on the bar and it bounded over to her, nearly knocking her over. She wrapped it in her arms and the squirming bundle of cute licked at every inch of her he could reach. His fur was like soft wire under her hands, and his big puppy paws dug into her. She didn't care.

"Stay." Dub's word echoed the one Shar uttered weeks ago. "Stay." He swallowed, and his eyes fell closed. "Please."

"I—" she didn't know what to say. She didn't *want* to go. But...

She sought out Mell and Shar. Mell had stopped bouncing, and both brothers looked at her with calm eyes. A tendril of emotion wrapped around her, and it was different. It was... real. An offering. It was a glimpse into the true Mell, instead of a construct. So often it was hard to tell, even for this goddess, but this time it was clear.

He offered her warmth and want and the exhilaration of their sing-songs. He offered her laughter and longing and shared pain. He offered her love.

Tears gathered in her eyes as the puppy licked at her chin.

Shar placed his hands on the bar, palm down. "I have already said how I feel. I want you to stay, but it is your decision. We do not care if you are a goddess, or a human, or a creature that will be our doom." He let out a soft chuckle. "If you have not figured it out yet, the Irish love a good tragedy. Even if you *were* our doom, we would embrace you." He ducked down until they were eye to eye, quite a feat for the giant. "But I do not believe you are our end. More like our beginning."

A phrase came to her, one from the Idiot's Guide. Kissed the Blarney Stone. *These brothers must have made love to the damn thing.*

Dub moved then, jumping over the bar, narrowly missing the back shelves and threatening to send the bottles of liquor to the floor. He stood before her and for once his face was not angry. It was soft, filled with something she wasn't ready to acknowledge as love, but may have been on the verge of it. Affection. *Let us call it affection and leave it there.*

He reached out and placed a hand on the puppy's head, stilling the little guy's movements.

"*Beag realta.* Little goddess." He smiled at her, soft and affectionate.

Bat's breath caught. She had seen this. It was her vision. The name she couldn't hear...

"Bat of the two faces, who has stirred up my home, and then brought it some balance. Bat, who has turned this pub into a sanctuary, and offered comfort to the weary. Bat, who has sought justice for one that most gods would consider insignificant. Not to find a soul blade, or stop someone from gaining power they should not have, but simply because she felt some kindness toward a leprechaun."

The name she couldn't hear before was her own.

"Please stay with us. We come to you as supplicants, and offer this small life to you, as both a protector and a companion." He drew in a breath. "We offer ourselves as protectors and companions, and we ask that you remain here, making this your new home. We offer up this place, this building, as a temple and a refuge." His smile turned into a small grin. "Just don't tell the Morrigan or we all get kicked out."

He stood before her, proud and straight, with strength and yearning a beautiful mix on his face. A warrior, as he once was, and as he would always be.

Bat swallowed and closed her eyes. Could she leave behind all that she was in her own land? All that she had been? A vacation, a break from the tedium and a taste of peace that was one thing. But to abandon her place in Egypt completely? Because that was what she would be doing. If she accepted their offer, she would leave all of her past behind and start anew. Did she want that? Wasn't that what she had really hoped for when she came here?

Yes.

Tightening her grip on her newest offering, she opened her eyes and met the shining lapis of Dub's gaze, then Shar's, then the soft brown of Mell's. "I accept this offering as worthy, and I grant your request."

And just as it had when she first stepped over the threshold, the world shifted.

For better or worse, she had a new home. One filled with warmth and comfort, music and laughter. Filled with beings that were, for the most part, abandoned and forgotten by their own gods; filled with those who had been served badly, or not at all, by absent gods.

She stepped up to Dub and freed one hand to hook around the back of his neck. She pulled him down and bestowed a soft kiss on his firm lips. "Thank you."

"Thank *you*, goddess. And welcome home."

Yes, she was, was she not?

Home.

A soft knock came from the door. The puppy wiggled in her arms, and she set him down as Mell unlocked and opened the door. Finn entered, his expression hard, and Bat's chest tightened. Things had been going so well.

Then she noted the guardi did not wear his uniform, and there were dark circles under his eyes still. He held a small case, just the right shape for...

"I thought I might play with you for a bit tonight. Unless you have another fiddler." He half held up the case, an aborted movement, and looked ready to bolt right out the door given the least provocation. "I'm not nearly as good as Oisin, or Dano, but I can hold my own."

Mell clasped his shoulder as Killer—*yes, that is a very good name for my new puppy*—sniffed Finn's shoes, growled, then wagged his tail.

Bat smiled, keeping it gentle. She wondered if the Morrigan, or another deity, had come to him, tried to help him after Grainne was killed by the soul blade. Per Ailis, it had almost appeared as though the woman had thrown herself on the blade. Or, she had attacked and Finn had done what he needed to.

"I would love to play a song or two with you, Finn."

He nodded, rolled his shoulders, and slumped into a stool closest to the door. The same one he'd sat in the night the Morrigan came to the pub, and again the night after. It wasn't claimed by any of the regulars yet.

She caught Dub's gaze and raised her brows, tilting her head to the stool. He frowned the frown that said he agreed, and nodded. They'd keep that seat open for Finn, then.

Shar disappeared as she busied herself pulling Finn a pint. She set it before the guardi captain—no, not tonight. This evening, he was just a not-man. Finn nodded and his lips quirked. She patted his hand.

When she turned to move away, he captured her hand. Killer jumped up and growled, but he didn't attack. Her puppy didn't know if the move was aggressive or not. Neither did Bat.

"Thank you, again," Finn said. He opened his mouth to say more, but the words didn't come.

Bat studied him, looking past the weariness, the red-gold hair that needed a trim, the dim colors of his eyes. She didn't have the same skills as Mell or Ailis with emotion, but she'd noted something in the last two weeks. The same ability to sense the *wrong* that she'd felt around Grainne had grown so that if she concentrated, she could find the seeds in others. It took a lot from her, and there was almost no range to speak of, the ability was new and unwieldy, but it was there. There had been two patrons, humans, she'd had thrown out because of it already.

Now, she looked deep into Finn. There were... holes in him. Areas of blank nothing, as though something had been ripped out.

But there was nothing of the chaos that Grainne had planted. Nothing of the poison, or whispered ideas of power and false love.

She gave his fingers a squeeze. "Be sure to come in more often. I know the guys would like to see more of you." She offered another smile. "And so would I."

THE MORRIGAN

She faced the Tribunal. This century the Dagda presided, Lugh and Danu on either side. The meeting room was informal, housed in a modest house in a little town near old Tara.

"It is done," she reported. She crossed her arms and paced to the widows. She hadn't bothered to sit when they'd invited her to. This was not a social visit, despite the pretensions of her fellow deities. "Was it really necessary?" While she was glad Grainne was finally done away with, she had not enjoyed witnessing Finn fumble with his own doubts.

The gods had, of course, known where the woman and

the blade had been the whole time. But it was vital it not be retrieved until the Unifier appeared, just as it was important for Finn to have killed Grainne himself, made that choice. If she'd stepped in…

"You know what Ruith predicted," the Dagda said. "And she has confirmed now is the time."

The Morrigan sniffed. She'd never liked that pretentious woman, but she couldn't deny the accuracy of the Druid's predictions. "You know I enjoy a good war, live for them, really," she flashed a smile and Danu shifted, frowning. "But I do not like my side to be unprepared."

Lugh sat forward, and the Dagda held up a hand stalling the Bright God. "Knowledge of what is to come will allow *us* to prepare properly. We know the players, and the way the pieces will need to move."

The Morrigan bowed her head in acknowledgment. Yes, this was a time that they all needed to move carefully. But there were ways she could nudge her warriors in the direction they needed to go, additional help she could provide.

It would have to be enough. For now.

She just hoped this forgotten goddess that had traveled to her land was ready for what was to come.

The next in the Forgotten Trilogy, The Legends That Remain, is now Available

A Note From the Author

~

I had way too much fun researching the background for this story.

It was interesting to note that both the Egyptian gods and the Irish gods were much less codified than those in other histories. Names and the roles of the gods shifted by time period and location.

Many elements are my own creation, and many are borrowed from various texts and books I found, including, yes, the Idiot's Guide to Irish History. I apologize for any inaccuracies... but let's just pretend it's right and roll with it, shall we?

Finn, as you may have guessed, was based on Fionn mac Cumhaill of the Fianna, and Diarmuid and Grainne really did run away with each other. The rest I took... liberties with.

Bat was a goddess of pre-dynastic Egypt, and some speculate that it was her shown on the Narmer palette between Horus and Set, uniting the Upper and Lower Kingdoms. She held many of the same qualities as Hathor and was eventually absorbed as just another aspect of that more popular goddess. She is also mentioned briefly in the pyramid texts.

Alatrom really was a Fomoiri, mentioned in the tales of Cu Chulainn. He had three sons, Dub, Mell and Dubros, who were seeking to take a maiden that Cu

Chulainn then rescued. It was said the hero killed them. I say *they* let *him* get away.

I took a little liberty with the last brother, changing his name to Searbhan. But, Searbhan was also another Fiomoiri I found, a one-eyed giant who guarded a sacred rowan in the time of the Fianna.

Who's to say they weren't really the same man?

Another note on their names. Dub means "dark". I found references for Mell as well, meaning either "dark" or "joy", "mild" and "pleasant" depending on sources. Interesting...

About the Author

Cecilia Randell was born in Austin, Texas and grew up in a home with her very own Cheerful Bulldozer. After some brief adventures in various places such as California and Florida, she returned to her hometown and took up a career in drafting.

A lifetime lover of words and stories, the transition to writing was two-fold: a comment from a relative and a short line from another author, saying to write what you want to read.

And thus the new adventure was born.

Now she can be found most days curled up in a comfy chair and creating new tales to share with others.

www.ingramcontent.com/pod-product-compliance
Lightning Source LLC
Chambersburg PA
CBHW021951170626
46808CB00001B/111